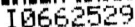

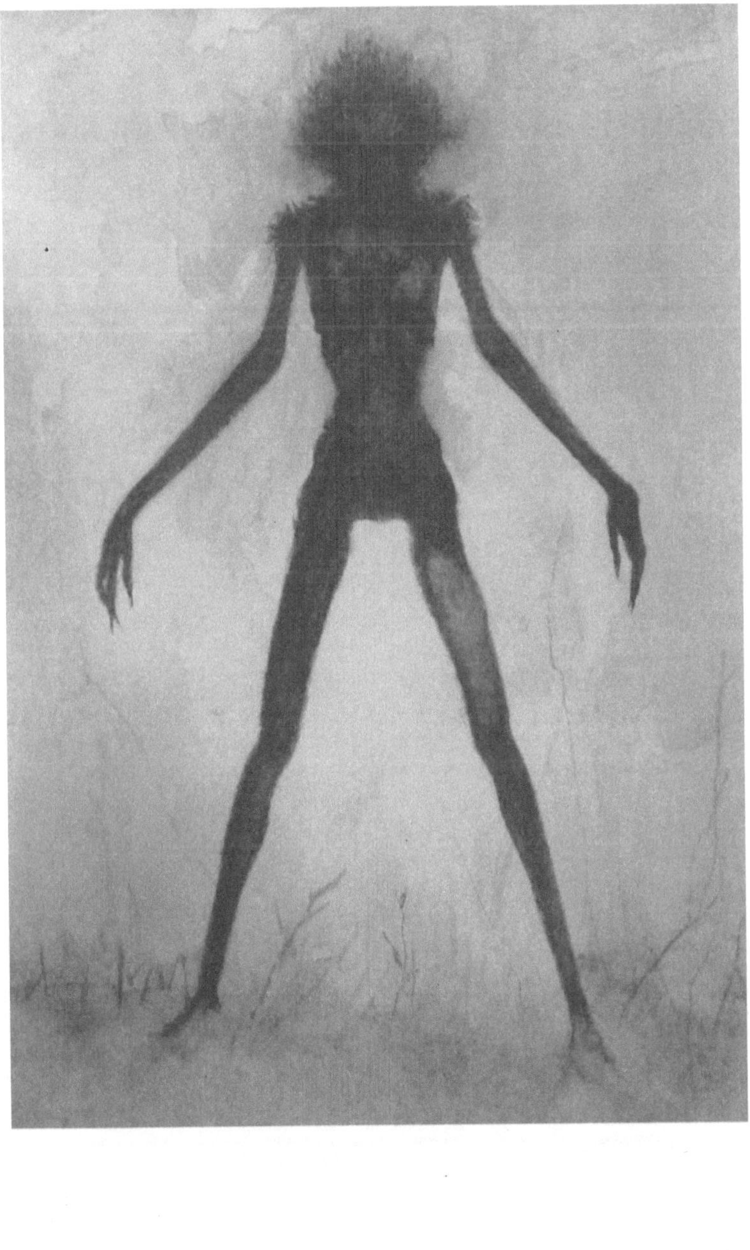

Soul Umbra

Juliet Rose

Above the Rain Collective

Above the Rain Collective

abovetheraincollective@gmail.com

North Georgia, USA

Contributing Editor: J.A. Sexton

Publisher's note:

This is a work of fiction. All characters and incidents are the product of the author's imagination, places are used fictitiously and any resemblance to an actual person, living or dead, is entirely coincidental.

ISBN: 979-8-9933717-0-2

First Printing December 2025

abovetheraincollective.com

authorjulietrose.com

Cover graphics and interior formatting by J.A. Sexton

Original cover photo by Sian Shurley

Above the Rain Collective logo artwork by Bee Freitag

May you heal from the things you don't talk about

Contents

Prologue

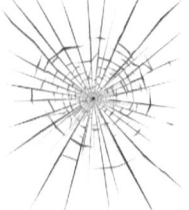

*A*lmost every neighborhood has one. An old lady the children are convinced is a witch who will eat them, one the parents find a little strange but simply avoid talking to. Sometimes the script changes slightly, but it's always an old person who's evil or ill-intentioned in their eyes. Never mind, they all get old, or these people are probably simply lonely and isolated. Nope, it has to be a witch. Hide the cats, don't make eye contact, don't venture too close, or she might grab the children. Turn them into soup.

This is a story of such a woman. The Witch of Magnolia Lane, as the neighborhood children called her. No one knew how long she'd been there, or who she was, but they all believed she was mad in the head. When she came out to shuffle down the driveway in her slippers, with a scowl on her face, to check the mail, the children all ran away screaming.

Their parents didn't stop them, either.

In some sick way, they all seemed to take delight in the old woman's reality. In her suffering. Everyone loves a pariah, a neighborhood tale to share in whispers at backyard barbeques and birthday parties. A story to keep the children from wandering too far, from challenging too much. So she shuffled back amid the screams and finger-pointing, her rolled-up stockings falling down to her thin and spotted ankles. To a home it seemed almost no one visited, and no one saw inside. Then, she was gone again until her next required outside excursion.

One day, she would be gone like the dust coating her windowsills and would be nothing more than a story the then-grown-up children told their own birthed gremlins. There was always a new witch to be had. A fresh tale to tell.

A completely lived life reduced to nothing more than aging and isolation. Lack of compassion wrapped in a story to tell around the fire amidst screams and giggles.

Sit down and get comfortable to hear her tale. The true story of the Witch of Magnolia Lane.

Chapter One

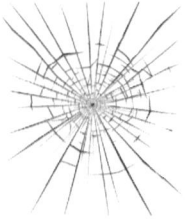

Blood saturated the sheets as the young mother took her last breaths. Her bereft husband cradled the squalling infant as his eyes beseeched the midwife to do something to save his beloved. The midwife moved with haste, trying everything to bring the dewy-faced girl back to life. It was for naught, however. The man was made a father and a widower in the same moment. He crumpled against the wall, holding the baby against his chest as his eyes ran with tears.

The baby, unaware of her mother's passing, kicked and squirmed in the thin blanket, wanting for the mother she no longer had. This set into motion a feeling of emptiness she never would be able to explain to anyone. Her father loved her and took care of her, but he, too, felt the hollow ache and could do little more than be kind and protective.

"Esme," he whispered into her small, red face, as he watched the blood run from his wife's body. "I'm so sorry."

Esme, unaware of what had transpired, stared up into his face and grunted. In later years, she would say she remembered being born, but most people chalked that up to her delusions. Poor crazy Esme, always telling some strange account of history that was hard to believe.

That day, however, her father placed her in the cradle beside his bed and rocked her as sobs overtook his body. He'd failed his wife. His body had caused her to die. His primal need to be completely within her. To make them one. To bring forth a life they together created.

Now, he was alone forever.

Esme, sensing his grief, began to cry. He gathered her into the bed with him, attempting to find comfort in the only family he had left. Esme, on the other hand, needed her mother's milk and wailed at the constraint of her father's arms. It felt like a prison, and her tiny arms beat against the love he was giving.

The man fell into a state of survival. He tended to his daughter, he went to work, and he made sure food was on the table. People pushed him to remarry, to give the girl a mother. To which he would shake his head and say he was all the child needed.

To a point, it was true as he made sure she never went without, but he unintentionally set her up for a lifetime of always sensing something was missing in her life. She never could put her finger on it, but everywhere she went, every person she met, she'd say, "No, that's not it." Not knowing what the *it* was, she was searching for.

Every night, the man would rock the baby and sing the lullabies he remembered his wife singing to her belly. This caused a splinter in Esme's brain, despite her father's good intentions. She knew the songs, but not the voice. She felt betrayed, and even from hearing them, Esme created a version of her mother to live with.

To find comfort in.

Her father lived on the outside, but this version of her mother lived on the inside. In her psyche, Esme would retreat to find the affection she so desired. Her father always felt when he stared into her small eyes that she wasn't all there. Or part of her judged him for letting his wife die. For letting her mother die. He took the shame because it was also his guilt. His burden to bear.

Maybe to a degree that was true. Esme often recounted in her later years how she always felt let down by her father. When asked why, she'd shake her head and sigh. "It was as if he held part of me away from myself."

After the first few weeks since his wife's death, the man finally let extended family visit the baby. He didn't want them there, but didn't feel it was fair to Esme to have only him in her life. So he opened the doors to his mother and sister, and they brought their broods, as well. Soon, the house was loud and chaotic with children running everywhere. His sister had four and no issues with bringing them into the world. She bounced back like she'd simply taken a walk.

This made him jealous. Angry even.

His mother doted on him, trying to replace his wife, and he resented her for it. Her attempts at coddling him only made him bitter and disgusted at her efforts. His sister went on and on about how he needed to come out of his grief and consider meeting someone new..

"It's better for Esme, she needs a mother. It's time to put away the sorrow and roll out the joy," she insisted as she used one of his wife's heirloom napkins to wipe some substance from her youngest's face.

He flinched but remained silent. There was no point in arguing back. His wife was barely cold in the ground, and they wanted him to move on. Not for him, though. Not for Esme, either. For their own comfort. Their ideas of family.

Finally, they gathered their things and left, promising to visit again soon. He made sure they didn't as long as he had a say in the matter. He didn't want them poisoning Esme against her mother. Erasing the memory and history of the one person who wanted Esme in the world than any of them. Being a mother was everything she'd longed for. He loved his wife, and she loved their daughter, so he loved their daughter. It didn't come naturally at first, but in time, she was all he cared about. So much so, Esme felt smothered and retreated more into her psyche than outside of herself.

Her father seemed to sense this by the time she was a toddler and could no longer fight the demons tormenting him day and night. He watched his dark, curly-haired, round-faced daughter play with toys on the floor and knew he couldn't face her disappointment anymore. He was the reason she was motherless. He was the reason she rarely smiled and never laughed. Not only had he failed the love of his life, he'd failed his daughter, as well.

The next day, he walked over to a neighbor and asked them to watch Esme for a bit while he did some interior painting in the house. He didn't want the little girl around all the fumes until it dried. He'd air it out before he came back to her. *No later than dinner time,* he promised. The neighbors had a little boy around the same age and were more than willing to let the quiet little girl stay and play. She'd be no trouble at all, they assured the father.

However, once dinner passed and he hadn't returned, the boy's father walked over to see if, possibly, Esme's father had fallen asleep after painting, or if the fumes had gotten to him. He knocked, but no answer came, so he pushed the door open and called in, "Hello, it's your neighbor! Are you alright? Hello? I'm coming in."

What he found in the house that day chilled him to the bone and gave him nightmares for the rest of his life. Esme's father was curled up in bed holding his late wife's nightgown against his chest with one hand. The other hand clutched a pistol. His brains were splattered all over the bed and the wall. The same bed where his wife had taken her last breath and ended any chance at joy for the small family.

A note beside him simply read. "I'm sorry, Esme."

Chapter Two

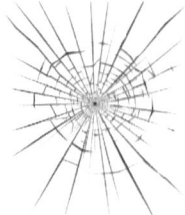

One of Esme's first memories was playing in her aunt's backyard with a stick and a ball when she was two or three. Her mother's sister. Her father's family didn't want anything to do with her. Her mother's older sister, Darla, took her in after her father's suicide, and while they treated her well, she always knew she wasn't theirs. They had older children who, by the time Esme showed up, had said goodbye to their childhoods and were more concerned with going out and away from the constraints of home. Away from family ties and the requirements that came with those bonds.

This left Esme by herself much of the time. Her aunt Darla made sure Esme's needs were met, but had moved on from mothering as her children pushed her away. She was loving but distant at times, leaving Esme learned to entertain herself. Esme was a quiet and undemanding child, so she played alone and didn't know any different.

That was until that day. Esme was pushing the ball with the stick when a young boy stepped out of the woods. He was a couple of years older than the young girl and had a head full of thick, dark hair that fell over his large, brown eyes. His face was kind, and he appeared there like he was meant to be.

Esme stopped playing and watched the boy. He waved his hand in a shy wave, and she waved back, happy to see someone close to her age. He walked over and picked up a stick, nudging the ball with it. Before long, they were batting the ball back and forth with their sticks and laughing. Esme didn't think to ask the boy's name, and when her aunt called her in for lunch, he disappeared back into the trees as if he'd never been there.

The boy showed up often for a couple of years after, and Esme called him "Gogo," though she wasn't sure why. He was her only friend until she reached school age, and he always showed up when she went outside to play. One day at dinner, she told her aunt about Gogo.

"Me and Gogo collected tadpoles today," she explained between bites of food. "We let them go, though. They were wiggly and hard to hold. "

Her aunt tipped her head, her brow furrowed. "Gogo? Who's that?"

"My friend. He comes when I play out back."

A look passed between Esme's aunt and uncle. Her aunt leaned forward, watching Esme intently. "What does this boy look like?"

Esme described Gogo the best she could in her limited child language. Her aunt listened with a frown. Once Esme was done, her aunt shook her head in confusion. "Honey, that doesn't make any sense. We don't have any children your age around here, and the boy sounds too young to be out wandering on his own."

Esme had no reply to that because how could she deny the boy who came to see her almost every day? He was her friend, and she played with him. She focused on her plate and let it drop. Later that evening, she could hear her aunt and uncle in what sounded like a tense conversation.

"That child needs something we can't give her," her uncle said. "She is making up imaginary friends to play with because she is so lonely. It's not fair to her."

A moment of silence was followed by what sounded like crying. Finally, her aunt spoke. "What choice do we have? She has no one. No one but us, Ray. Once she starts school, it will get better. She'll have lots of friends and will forget about the made-up boy."

More mumbling followed by more crying, and Esme retreated into her closet. It was the place she felt most at peace. She curled up with a teddy bear and fell asleep. At some point in the night, she felt arms lift her and carry her to her bed. Esme peered up at her uncle, who seemed sad.

He read her Goldilocks and the Three Bears. Once he was done, he sat on the edge of her bed and ran his hand through his thinning hair. "Esme, I need you to be careful who you talk to. Your imaginary friend Gogo doesn't ever ask you to leave or do something you shouldn't, right? He doesn't ask you questions about us, does he?"

Esme shook her head, her golden curls bouncing against he cheek. "Gogo is real."

Her uncle sighed and stared off. "Alright. He's real to you, I understand that. Does he ever ask you to do something you shouldn't?"

"No, we just play."

Her uncle tucked the blanket around Esme and nodded. "If anyone ever asks you to go with them, you know not to, right? You always come and talk to your aunt or me. Do you understand?"

Esme wasn't sure why they seemed upset by her friend, and she rubbed her small nose. "Okay. We just play in the yard, Uncle Ray."

"Esme, we have never seen your friend in the yard. We see you playing out there all the time by yourself. It's okay if you made him up, but if someone is coming in the yard, we need to know."

Esme yawned and turned over in her bed, tired of the conversation. "Good night."

Her uncle got up to leave and paused at the door, breathing heavily. She didn't understand why, but he seemed upset about Gogo.

By the next morning, Esme forgot all about their talk and went to play as usual. This time, though, Gogo didn't show up. Esme watched the tree line in the hopes her friend would come play, however, he didn't come. Disappointed, she played by herself and kept checking the trees for his shadow. He didn't come for weeks, and she almost gave up when, one rainy day, she was drawing on the back porch when a rustling in the woods got her attention.

Esme climbed off the porch and let her tiny legs carry her across the yard. When she made it to the trees, the rain had picked up, and her wet hair was getting in her eyes. She attempted to push it off her face and blinked away the water dripping down her face.

"Hello? Gogo?" she called out into the dark woods.

At first, it was silent, then a giggle erupted from behind a tree, startling her. Esme stopped closer to the tree and saw a small hand holding onto the bark. She reached out to touch it, and Gogo appeared from behind the tree.

"You found me!" he exclaimed.

They darted through the trees, even though the rain had soaked Esme to the bone and she was shivering. Somehow, Gogo seemed to stay dry. Exhaustion overtook Esme, so she lay down next to a tree trunk to rest for a moment. Gogo sang her nursery rhymes as she dozed off to sleep.

The sound of people calling out her name woke her up, and she realized it was dark out. She shivered uncontrollably and was drenched all the way through her clothing. She attempted to sit up, but her body was too cold. Too stiff. Gogo was nowhere around. He must have gone home.

Lights were bouncing around the trees, and a large man came through the woods. He spied her and called out. "Hey! Over here!"

Within seconds, Esme was surrounded by a slew of people. Her aunt busted through the crowd and ran to Esme's side, scooping the freezing child up. Aunt Darla clutched Esme to her chest and ran.

Esme didn't remember much else, but she woke up in the hospital, and her aunt and uncle were upset she had wandered away. She'd been missing for hours, and the authorities were called out to find her. The whole neighborhood was searching for the little girl and feared the worst had happened. That she'd been kidnapped or drowned in a nearby pond. When Esme tried to explain she was only playing with Gogo, her aunt blew up.

"Stop it! We were so worried about you, Esme. Everyone dropped what they were doing to find you. The whole neighborhood was looking for you and judging us for losing you. No more talk of your imaginary friend!" she yelled through tears.

Esme retreated inside herself. She didn't want her aunt to be angry, but Gogo was real. He was her friend. She decided she wouldn't talk about him to them ever again, not to anyone. She would play with him and never tell a soul. He wasn't imaginary.

A few weeks later, after she'd recovered, Esme was looking at picture albums in her aunt's den. She still wasn't allowed to go outside, but her aunt let her play in the den and said she was fine to look at any of the albums on the bottom shelf. Esme flipped through the books, not recognizing anyone but still finding the pictures interesting. Pictures of holidays and parties, adults and children frozen in time

Esme flipped to a page with faded photos and stopped. One picture showed children on a shoreline, building a sand castle. One of the boys was looking up into the camera with a mischievous grin. His dark hair fell over his large brown eyes.

Gogo.

Esme frowned. Not only was Gogo real, he was in her aunt's picture albums. Why did they pretend he didn't exist? She patted the photo and smiled. Gogo smiled back. Esme stood up, gathered the large book in her short arms, and wandered clumsily to the kitchen with it to show her aunt.

Aunt Darla was sitting at the kitchen counter, smoking a cigarette and chatting on the phone. When she saw Esme come in with the album, she excused herself from the phone call and blotted out the cigarette.

"Whatcha' got there, hon?" she asked as Esme drew closer. "You enjoying looking at the photos?"

Esme came over and set the album on the floor, pointing at the black and white photo. "Gogo."

Her aunt frowned in confusion as she stared at the album. "I'm sorry, what are you saying?"

Esme pointed again. "It's my friend Gogo."

Her aunt picked up the album and peered closer, then eyed Esme, her face unreadable. "Esme, that's your daddy when he was a boy. These were the albums I took from your parents' home when you came here to live with us. I wanted you to know both sides of your family. See, that's his name written on the photo border right there."

Esme glanced at the photo and the scribbled name, her eyes landing on the one friend she'd had for the last couple of years. She shook her head with determination. She'd know that boy anywhere.

"No, Aunt Darla, that's my friend Gogo."

Chapter Three

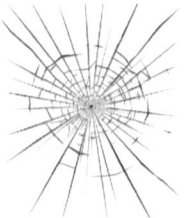

She never saw Gogo again. Her aunt decided it was time for Esme to start therapy, so once a week, she'd go and draw pictures and play games with a nice lady named Ruth. Esme liked these sessions and wasn't sure what therapy meant, but Ruth was fun to be around. She made silly voices and complimented every drawing Esme did, even the ones she didn't try her best on. Sometimes she even asked Esme to play make-believe and tell her what the people in the drawings were doing.

However, in one of the sessions, Ruth turned more serious, and five-year-old Esme was thrown off guard. Ruth seemed distracted, even worried about something. She set Esme's drawing aside and smiled, her eyes pained.

"This will be our last visit, Esme. You'll be starting school in a couple of months, and your Aunt Darla would like to take you on vacation out of state before then. I want to know you are a very special little girl. You are a bright and thoughtful child. I will miss seeing you, but I think you'll love going to school."

Esme felt a strange yet familiar feeling creeping into her chest and stared with blinking eyes. Like her parents, like Gogo, Ruth was another person to abandon her. To leave when she needed her most. Esme wanted to cry, but the tears wouldn't come. Instead, she put the feeling inside her tummy, shrugged, and simply said, "Okay."

Ruth looked like she wanted to say something else, but sighed. She glanced down at Esme's drawing and ran her fingers over the raised crayon lines. She smiled at Esme. "Would you like to draw me a picture I can hang on my wall in here, so I can see it and think of you?"

Esme grabbed the crayons and began drawing a picture for Ruth. While she was in the middle of her artwork, Aunt Darla came to the door, and Ruth asked to speak to her in private. Esme's aunt appeared uncomfortable but nodded, waving her hand.

"Of course."

"Let's step into my study for a moment. Esme is making me a picture to hang on my wall in here. Esme, your aunt, and I will be right in there talking for a moment. Knock if you need us, alright?"

Esme didn't look up but muttered, "Yes."

The door closed behind the women, and Esme peered around the room. Over the last couple of years, she'd been going there, she'd memorized every knick-knack, every ray of light coming in through the dusty wooden shutters, every photo on Ruth's desk. She could draw it out of memory. Maybe when she got home, she'd draw a picture of Ruth's office to hang in her own room to think about being there, like she was doing for Ruth. That thought made her feel better about not coming back.

After a few minutes, she could hear raised voices emanating from the other room. Not yelling, but tense. Esme watched the door, expecting it to fling open, however, it remained closed. She went back to her drawing, whispering softly to herself. To the people in her picture.

When Ruth and Aunt Darla finally emerged, Ruth appeared like she'd been crying, and Esme's aunt had red splotches on her cheek like when she got mad about something. Her aunt came over and stood behind Esme, her hand on the girl's shoulder, anxious to leave. Esme wasn't done with her drawing, though, and ignored her aunt's passive attempt at getting her attention.

The air in the room had changed, and Esme glanced around. It all looked the same, but it felt different somehow. Ruth sat down at her desk and began scribbling notes in Esme's file. She closed the folder and got up to make copies of what was in there in the other room. Esme didn't like how things felt and started rocking back and forth and humming to settle her worry.

"Stop that, Esme," her aunt whispered, the words harsher than how she usually spoke.

Esme had the sense of a veil being raised inside herself and pressed the crayon hard to the picture, snapping it in half. Ruth came back and stared between her patient and the aunt. The tension in the air was almost electric, and she didn't want to leave things that way. Ruth frowned and placed her hand over Esme's.

"It's okay. People who come into your life always live within you. They remain part of you for life. I asked your aunt if you could come visit sometimes, but she thinks it's best if you start school and focus on friends your age. I think you'll love school and make wonderful friends."

Esme glanced up and met Ruth's eyes, seeing the truth in them. She was worried about Esme going to school. She was concerned about Esme not coming back for therapy. Ruth was simply agreeing with Aunt Darla because otherwise Esme would feel torn in two, and Ruth didn't want to be the cause of that. What Ruth didn't know was Esme already felt that way; she always had. Or maybe Ruth did know, because sometimes she asked Esme about her inner self versus her outer self. Ruth seemed to know a lot.

Esme finished the drawing and stood up, clutching it in her hand. She wasn't ready to leave, but her aunt was shuffling her toward the door without looking back. Esme pushed her aunt away and ran over to hug Ruth, shocking all three of them. Esme was not a physically affectionate child by any means, and this show of intimacy was unheard of.

Ruth knelt down and wrapped her arms around Esme. "I am very proud of you, Esme. Thank you for coming to see me. I will miss you."

Esme let go and stepped back, holding out the drawing which had been formed into a roll her her hands. Ruth smiled and took it, setting it on her desk. She handed Esme's aunt a folder of copied documents and nodded, her mouth in a grim line. "If you feel Esme could benefit from seeing me again, I will accept her back at any time. I wish you would give some serious thought to what we discussed."

Esme didn't understand what they were talking about, but from the way her aunt's body stiffened, Esme knew she'd never be back to see Ruth. Her aunt took Esme's hand and cleared her throat.

"We appreciate the time and concern you've given Esme over these last two years. We can see how much she liked coming to see you. It's time for a new chapter in her life now."

Before Ruth could respond, Aunt Darla guided Esme out of the room, through the lobby, and down the stairs. Esme glanced back up at the tall building and stared at one of the windows. She raised her hand in a wave, and her aunt looked at where she was waving.

"Who are you waving at, Esme?"

Esme remained silent and dropped her eyes. They got to the truck, and Darla opened the door for Esme, helping her step up into the vehicle. Esme settled in and stared out the window as her aunt went around to the other side. She climbed in and let out a deep breath, turning to Esme.

"I'm sorry. I know how much you liked Ruth. She was very good to you. Life is changing, and we need to adapt. You start kindergarten in about six weeks, and your uncle and I thought it would be nice to take a long trip to the beach. Your cousins don't want to go because they want to hang out with their friends, so we thought it would be fun for the three of us to go. Does that sound fun?"

Esme smiled and nodded her head. It *did* sound fun. They'd been to the beach the summer before for a few days, and Esme had been mesmerized by the ocean. By the constant waves coming in over and over. She hadn't wanted to leave then. Now it sounded like they'd be staying much longer. Excitement bubbled in her chest.

"Can we go to the arcade?" she asked, remembering the beachside arcade they played in the year before. Her favorite game was skeeball.

"Of course! We can get ice cream at that little shop on the strand, too. It will be so much fun, Esme," her aunt replied, seeming like her old self again. Relieved even.

Esme was happy to feel the tension release. She didn't like it when the adults around her were unhappy with each other. She began humming, this time out of peace. Her aunt started the truck and clicked on the radio. She began to back out of the space and hit her brakes all of a sudden. Esme jerked forward in the seat, the belt catching her from flying into the dashboard.

"What the hell is she doing?" her aunt muttered and put the truck back in park.

Ruth came around the driver's side and rapped on the window, her eyes large and concerned. Aunt Darla rolled the window down and stared at the clearly stressed therapist.

"I need to talk to you a moment," Ruth whispered.

Esme noticed Ruth was holding her drawing in her hand, and worry washed over her. Was she in trouble?

Darla reluctantly got out, and the two women walked away from the truck. Esme could see Ruth was showing her aunt the drawing, and the sensation in her gut returned. Darla was peering at the picture with her hand to her mouth, then she glanced at Esme sitting in the truck.

After a few minutes, the women came over to Esme's side. Ruth smiled at her. "Thank you so much for the drawing, Esme.

I can tell you took a lot of time on all the details. So I know, can you tell me who is in this picture?"

Esme took the picture and pointed to the different people she drew. "That's Uncle Ray and Aunt Darla. These two are my cousins, John and Becky. This is my mom and dad in heaven."

Ruth smiled in encouragement. "Is that you?" she asked, pointing to a little girl in a blue dress.

Esme nodded and touched the picture where she'd drawn a little boy figure. "That's Gogo."

"Who is this, then?" Darla interjected, pointing to a tall, thin man wearing only gray clothing. His face was mostly covered by a hood, but a gaunt chin stuck out from it. In the picture, he was holding Esme's hand, his gangly fingers around hers. Like a vice.

She didn't want to answer. They wouldn't understand if she told them. Her aunt had made Gogo disappear already. However, they watched her intently, letting her know she needed to answer the question. She glanced at the picture.

"That's Tall Man."

"Who is Tall Man, Esme?" Ruth asked gently, encouraging Esme to let them know.

Aunt Darla watched like a hawk, her face not hiding the fact that she was displeased with the drawing. Esme didn't want her aunt to be mad at her, but she knew she shouldn't lie. She rubbed her nose and spoke softly.

"He stands by my bed at night. He's everywhere I am."

Chapter Four

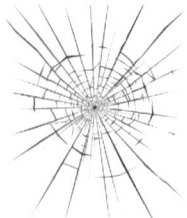

The first time Tall Man showed up was not long after Gogo went away for good. Esme was distraught over the loss of her only friend and withdrew into herself. She blamed her aunt and uncle for Gogo's disappearance and wished herself dead so they would suffer for causing her such great pain. She'd imagine them finding her dead body and cursing themselves for their cruelty. It was one of those nights, as she cried herself to sleep, she noticed a shadow in the far corner of her room. At first, she thought it was from the door being slightly cracked open, creating a stream of brightness from the hallway light.

Then, she recognized the shadow as something separate from anything in the room or house. It moved in a detached way, like a man standing in the room, but as if he was part of a different reality. There but not there. Esme sat up in bed and pushed her tear-wet hair out of her face.

"Who are you?" she asked with trepidation, a little afraid, yet a little intrigued.

The figure didn't speak but stepped into the stream of light coming from the hall through the partially opened door. Esme squinted and sucked in her breath. It *was* a man. Sort of. He was tall and thin, semi-transparent like a shadow or ghost. Where his eyes should have been were two dark orbs with moving sparks of light, like his eye sockets held the galaxy.

Esme stared at this new presence. Her skin felt crawly as if she should be scared, however, she wasn't. Not totally. The man came closer and reached out with his long, angular arm. His fingers seemed to stretch toward her like they were made of smoke, and Esme couldn't resist the urge to touch them. As she placed her hand in the curling wisps of his appendages, she saw her life until that moment. Her birth, her mother's death, her first steps, her father's suicide. She even saw herself through Gogo's eyes. No end and no beginning.

"Who are you?" she repeated, but the tall man didn't answer. Not with words, anyway. He communicated by placing thoughts in her mind. Esme came to understand she'd called him to her. In her anger and her grief, she'd opened the door and invited him in.

Esme lay down and pulled her covers to her chin with a smile. The figure stood by her bed, its shape constantly shifting like water. "I'll call you Tall Man," Esme whispered and drifted off to sleep, finding peace in the presence.

From that point forward, Tall Man came every night and stood by her bed. Esme missed Gogo, but Tall Man helped her feel less alone. She never told her aunt and uncle. She never told anyone. Not even Ruth when she started therapy. Telling people meant her friends went away.

She didn't think Ruth would notice when she drew Tall Man on the last day of therapy. Especially since she drew what Tall Man showed her parents to look like, and she included them. Gogo, too. Esme created a family picture. Gogo and Tall Man were part of her family.

The fallout that ensued from the drawing made Esme determined never to trust another adult again. Or anyone. Ruth shouldn't have shown Aunt Darla the private drawing made only for her. Esme drew it, believing Ruth would understand and keep her secret.

Instead, she betrayed her.

They never went to the beach after that. Esme's aunt and uncle, convinced the little girl was having a mental breakdown, agreed to have her go to a special hospital for a month. They told her the people there would help her. Esme knew better. Tall Man told her so. They would try to make him go away like Gogo.

Everyone in the hospital spoke to Esme as if she were dumb. Soft, high-pitched voices. Asking her if she needed this or that. Having her play silly games and draw pictures to try to expose her secrets. She did what they wanted, however, she kept the truth deep inside. She drew pictures of her aunt and uncle, cousins, even pets. But never Tall Man or Gogo. Not again.

At the end of the month, she told a lie. One that hurt her heart and made her ashamed as soon as it came out of her mouth. Her doctor, Mr. Ben, sat her down and asked her questions about the upcoming school year, about her favorite toys, about her cousins, about Gogo.

About Tall Man.

"He doesn't come see me anymore," Esme answered, dropping her eyes to stare at her hands. "He went away."

Dr. Ben watched her and smiled. "How does that make you feel. Do you miss him?"

Esme shook her head, holding her chin up. "No. I am ready to go to school and meet friends."

She met Dr. Ben's eyes, and he seemed to be considering what she'd told him. He tapped his pen against a pad of paper on his desk and leaned forward. "School should be fun. What happens if Tall Man comes back? Will you let your aunt and uncle know?"

Esme stared past Dr. Ben at the shifting dark shadow in the corner and nodded her head. "Yes, I will tell them."

Seeming satisfied, Dr. Ben offered her a piece of candy from a bowl on his desk and leaned back. "You are a very special little girl, Esme. You have a vivid imagination and are very bright. Maybe you can take that creativity and write some stories when you feel sad."

Tall Man warned her not to do that. Esme wriggled in her seat. "I have to use the bathroom."

"Of course, of course. Your aunt is on her way to take you home very soon. Why don't you go to the potty, then gather your things?"

She wasn't a baby and didn't like him calling the bathroom 'potty'. She got off the chair and waited, expecting him to say something else. When he didn't, she went out and walked down the hall to the bathroom. She didn't have to go, but had learned saying she needed to go to the bathroom got her out of just about any situation.

Esme slipped into the bathroom and locked the door. It was cool and dark in the bathroom, so she left the light off. She went to the sink and peered into the mirror, not recognizing the face staring back at her. She touched her cheek, then the other. In the reflection, she could see Tall Man standing behind her. Like he always was. He never spoke, but still communicated with her in his own way. Warning her of things. She focused on him instead of herself and felt safe.

Later, when her aunt came to get her to go home, Esme was sure to say the things they wanted to hear. Everyone seemed very excited about her going to school, even though she wasn't. Her aunt was quiet and helped Esme load her belongings into the car.

Once they were in the car, driving back home, Aunt Darla smiled at Esme. "We missed you. Your uncle painted your room, and we bought you a new bed set. It's very pretty. Pink, purple, and turquoise. We think you'll love it."

Esme listened but didn't know how to respond. She knew her aunt and uncle loved her, however, she still felt like they were in one room and she was in another. By the time they got home, Esme was tired and wanted to lie in her bed. She climbed the stairs up to her room after hugging everyone and pretending to be glad to be back.

The room was very bright and colorful. The bedspread had mermaids and happy fish. The walls were painted bright blue and pink. The curtains shimmered with purple and blue. Esme set her bag down and frowned. The room was cheery and fun. What every little girl would want.

She hated it.

At dinner, everyone acted like nothing happened. Aunt Darla promised to take Esme school shopping and to visit the school before the school year started. Esme acted excited and pushed her food around her plate, ignoring the gnawing in her gut. Her uncle was oddly quiet, and she eyed him across the table. He wouldn't make eye contact with her. She was different now.

At bedtime, her uncle surprised her by coming in to read a story. Esme climbed into bed and watched him. He picked a storybook from the shelf and sat on the edge of the bed. Esme could tell his heart wasn't in when, halfway through, he set the book down and looked at her.

"I'm sorry, Esme. I know you aren't happy here. Your aunt and I love you very much. I hope you know that. You need to let us in. We are trying. You used to be my special girl, but now..." he trailed off.

Esme didn't know what to say, but could sense his sadness. She placed her hand on his, and he smiled. He picked the book up and finished reading it. After he tucked her in and left, Esme was relieved when the lights went off and she didn't need to see the splashes of color and mermaids anymore.

As the darkness settled in, Esme saw Tall Man in the corner, like the first time they'd met. He seemed to have a heaviness about him, and Esme knew something was going to happen. Something bad. When Tall Man told her what her knew, she put another piece of stone on the wall.

Her uncle would be gone by morning.

Chapter Five

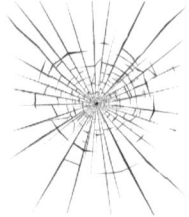

The screams that woke Esme would be ones she would hear in her mind until the day she died. Her aunt was screaming at the top of her lungs in a way Esme had never heard before. She stumbled out of bed to see what was happening, then she saw her aunt crouched over her uncle's still body. He was at the bottom of the stairs and blood was coming from his mouth. Esme stood frozen at the top of the stairs when her aunt peered up at Esme, her eyes frantic.

"Call 911!"

Esme didn't understand what that meant and ran past her aunt and uncle out the front door, heading for the neighbor's house. She bolted across the lawn, her bare feet slipping on the cool morning dew. One neighbor, Mr. Burton, was leaving for work, and she made a beeline for him. His eyes widened with shock when he saw the small girl speeding toward him in only her nightgown. He set his briefcase down and frowned.

"Is everything alright? Esme, is it?" he asked.

She ignored his questions and began speaking without breathing. "My uncle, he fell. He's bleeding at the bottom of the stairs. My aunt said to call someone. We need help. Please come help."

Mr. Burton stared for a moment, then caught sight of his wife at the front door. "Lisa, call an ambulance. It sounds like Ray took a tumble."

Lisa disappeared into the house, and Mr. Burton came over to Esme. "Let's get you back home. You shouldn't be out here in your pajamas and no shoes."

Esme stared down at her feet and felt a sense of shame, but she wasn't sure why. She let Mr. Burton take her hand and lead her back home. As they got to the front porch, they could hear sirens in the distance. Mr. Burton began to climb the steps, but Esme held back. She didn't want to go back in there. She didn't want to see Uncle Ray looking like that, with the blood and all.

"No," was all she said.

Mr. Burton stopped, then nodded. "I suppose not. Just sit right here and I'll see what's happening inside."

Esme sat on the cold wooden step as he slipped inside the front door. She could see flashing lights coming up the road, but knew it was too late. The ambulance skidded into the driveway and stopped as paramedics jumped out with their bags. They rushed past her as if she wasn't there.

Within minutes, they came back out and brought a gurney in. Wailing started from inside, and Esme shuddered, the sound bringing back a memory she couldn't quite form in her head.

However, she felt it. The pain. It could only mean one thing. Uncle Ray was dead. The paramedics came out, easing the gurney down the stairs, Aunt Darla following behind, sobbing into her hands.

Uncle Ray was strapped to the portable bed, a clear mask over his nose and mouth. He was still, but they were checking his vitals as they moved.

"I think I feel a faint pulse. Get the paddles ready," one of the paramedics stated as they moved past Esme. Once they were on level ground, one of them began chest compressions as they neared the ambulance. They slid the gurney into the back and climbed in, speeding off.

Aunt Darla stared at Esme for a moment like she didn't recognize her, then shook her head. "Fuck."

Esme didn't know why her aunt was upset with her and withdrew into herself a little more. She wrapped her small arms around her legs and made herself as small as she could. Her aunt went inside, then came out with her car keys.

"I need to go to the hospital. Becky is inside making calls to family about Ray. You can stay with her until I get back. Hopefully, they get your uncle feeling better again," she said, almost to herself as she headed for the car. "Yes, he'll be alright."

Esme watched her aunt leave, her car backing out and disappearing down the road. Her aunt was wrong. Uncle Ray was already gone. They were trying to revive an empty shell. Esme watched until she couldn't see the car anymore, then her eyes focused on what had been standing in the front yard the whole time. Invisible to everyone except Esme.

Tall Man.

His figure faded in and out as black tendrils floated off his body in delicate wisps. He also watched Aunt Darla leave, then turned back to the tiny girl on the steps. His hollow eyes gazed at her as she tried to convince herself it wasn't true.

It was.

Tall Man had something to do with Uncle Ray's situation. No, not situation. Death. Whether or not they wanted to admit it, Ray was gone. Esme stood up and turned her back on Tall Man. She didn't want to see him anymore. He wasn't her friend; he caused this. She began to climb the stairs to the house when Tall Man appeared in front of her, blocking her way into the house. He didn't speak to her, but he communicated, anyway.

He told Esme her uncle was a sacrifice to keep her safe. She didn't know from what and didn't want to hear anymore. Her uncle had always been kind to her, protected her, made her laugh. He was one of her favorite people in the world, and Tall Man took him away from her. Rage filled Esme, and she felt her face tingle with heat as she balled up her fists in anger.

"I hate you! I hate you! I hate you!" she screamed as hot tears rolled down her cheeks.

Tall Man moved toward her, and she jerked back, falling down the stairs. She hit each step with a thud and smacked her head against the concrete sidewalk below, blacking out.

When she came to, Becky was standing over Esme, her eyes panicked. When Esme's eyes fluttered open, Becky crouched down and held her head gently. "Thank God! I thought you were dead. What happened, Esme?"

Esme's head throbbed as she squinted up at Becky. "I fell down the steps."

"Well, obviously. How did you fall?"

Esme peered around, but Tall Man was gone. She couldn't tell Becky the truth. They would send her away again. "My feet were wet from the grass and I slipped."

"Jesus, Esme. We don't need two ambulances. Come on, let me help you inside and put some ice on your head. You have a knot back there. Mom is going to kill me for letting this happen when I was supposed to be watching you."

Becky had never paid so much attention to Esme, and it felt nice. Esme let Becky help her to her feet and guide her into the house. They went to the kitchen, and Becky sat Esme in a chair at the table. She checked the knot again and sighed.

"Damnit. Hold on, let me get you some ice for that."

Becky went to the freezer and frowned. She fished around for ice, but when she didn't find any, she grabbed a pack of frozen green beans, bringing them over to Esme. "There isn't any ice, put these on the back of your head."

Esme did as she was told and scanned around the kitchen. No Tall Man. All of a sudden, the phone rang, startling both girls. Becky groaned and went to answer it, turning her back to Esme. She began talking softly to the person on the other end of the line.

Esme slid off the chair, still clutching the green beans to the back of her head, and walked to the bottom of the stairs. A small pool of blood was where her uncle's body had been, and she bent down to look at it. It was once part of him, now a weird congealing puddle of nothing. It made her sad. At the same time, she found it fascinating in a way she couldn't quite put her finger on.

The sound of crying drew her attention, and she went back to the kitchen. Becky was sitting on the floor, cradling the phone in her lap. Her face was red and splotchy. Esme watched her cousin from the doorway, not sure what to do. Becky gazed up at her, her eyes empty.

"He's gone. Dad's dead."

Esme already knew that, but understood this was news to Becky. She went over and sat next to her cousin, placing her tiny hand in Becky's. Becky squeezed her hand and began sobbing. Now neither of them had a father.

"They said they think he had a cardiac episode, which made him fall down the stairs," Becky whispered. She wasn't really telling Esme, as much as she was saying it out loud to herself. To make the terrible news make sense.

Esme didn't know what a cardiac episode was, but she knew there was more to it than that. Tall Man had done something to hurt her uncle, she was sure of it. He'd forewarned her something bad was going to happen. Esme leaned her head against Becky's shoulder. They sat in silence until the phone began ringing again.

For the next few hours, Becky answered calls and made others. Esme dressed and sat watching the scene as if she wasn't part of it. Every now and then, Becky would check on her. Her other cousin, John, came home from work, and he and Becky talked in another room. He came out, his eyes red, and smiled weakly at Esme. They hadn't been close, but at the moment, they all felt the same detached, floating sensation as each other.

Aunt Darla came home briefly, gathered some paperwork, and left. She didn't speak to Esme or even seem to register she was there. Esme tried to stay out of the way and went to her bedroom to be alone and gather her thoughts. A book her uncle had read to her recently sat on the nightstand, and she began to flip through it, wishing he was in the other room. She thought about the funny voices he made when he read to her, and tears welled up in her eyes. She forced them down and shook her head.

Everyone left.

She wasn't sure when she dozed off, but woke up with her head pounding and disoriented. The house was quiet. She peered into the hallway and could see a light on in Becky's room. She padded down to her cousin's room and peered in. Becky had her head down on her desk and had fallen asleep that way. Esme checked on John, and he was reading in bed. He didn't notice her, so she went to her aunt and uncle's room. It was empty, and the bed was unslept in.

Esme went back to her room and walked over to the window. Aunt Darla's truck wasn't in the driveway. She hadn't come home from the hospital. Esme silently wept at the window, understanding nothing would be the same again. Death had once again visited her door, and she couldn't push away the feeling it was her fault.

As if she called him into being, Tall Man appeared under the window, his soulless eyes staring up at her. Seeking acceptance from Esme. Something she would never give again. She put her chin up and embraced the hatred in her heart.

"Go away! I never want to see you again."

So he did.

Chapter Six

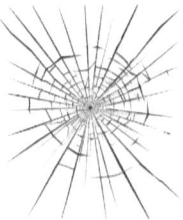

O ver the next few years, life fell into patterns. Not necessarily what one could call normal, but patterns nonetheless. Eating, sleeping, bathing, eating, sleeping, bathing, and so on. Esme went to school and lost her baby teeth. Becky graduated from high school, but chose to go to community college to stay home and take care of her mother. Aunt Darla was never the same after Ray's death and slowly drew inside herself. Her once bubbly nature was replaced with blank stares and early bedtimes. It was as if part of her died when Uncle Ray did.

Esme couldn't shake the guilt. Every time she saw Aunt Darla, she saw the ghost of Uncle Ray standing behind her. Not figuratively. Literally. He never spoke and never made eye contact, however, he was always there like a shadow. Esme tried to get his attention, but outside of Darla, he didn't seem aware of the rest of them. Not even his own children.

Only Aunt Darla.

Her cousin John left as soon as he graduated. Unlike Becky, he seemed like he couldn't wait to get away from the depressing home once and for all. He only came back on certain holidays, and even then made it clear he didn't want to be there. Aunt Darla didn't seem to notice, either way. Like Uncle Ray, she was a ghost in the home. Simply passing through rooms.

Becky became like a second mother to Esme, and as time went on, the young girl came to believe Becky was actually staying for her and not her mother. She never seemed resentful at the burden and made sure Esme had the things she needed to grow and survive. Together, they created a strange but sad little family.

By the time Esme was going into middle school, the bank came after the home. Without Ray working and Darla not even remembering bills were something she needed to be aware of, the home was far from being anything that could be saved. Becky now worked as a receptionist at a local medical clinic and tried her best to keep things together. However, the pit of debt was too much for her to handle alone, so she let the house go into foreclosure and moved the three of them to a two-bedroom apartment across town.

This meant Esme had to start a new school mid-year. Even though she'd been a loner at her old school, she'd grown up with the other children, and they accepted her as she was. Her new school wasn't as kind. Going into sixth grade halfway through as the strange new girl made her a target for every other child who wanted to make sure they weren't picked on. They set their sights on Esme and didn't let up.

The teasing was relentless and eventually turned into small but impactful physical abuse. Her lunch box was destroyed, her glasses broken. She was tripped and shoved in the hall. She found gum and wads of chewed-up paper in her wavy hair. Becky was stressed out trying to work and be a step-in mother, so Esme didn't tell her what was happening at school. Aunt Darla watched soap operas all day and didn't seem to notice Esme at all. Uncle Ray still hung around, though he seemed more see-through as the years went on. There but not there.

After one particularly cruel event, where Esme found a thick lock of her hair had been cut off at lunchtime, she went to the bathroom to cry. She often did this, tucking herself away in the farthest stall, the heel of her palm shoved in her mouth so no one could hear her sobs.

The bell rang for the children to go back to class, but Esme couldn't make herself leave the stall. The children would laugh at her chopped hair, even though they were the cause of it. She heard the halls quiet as the other kids made their way to class and held her breath. Her teacher would send someone to look for her if she didn't show up to class. Esme wiped her eyes and listened for the sound of footsteps.

The bathroom door creaked open, and she heard a soft patter of feet coming in her direction. She peered under the stall door and saw a pair of dingy white sneakers stop in front of the stall. Esme pulled her feet up to her chest on the toilet, balancing on the rim. Maybe they would leave if they thought she wasn't in there..

Instead, a soft knock came on the metal door. "Esme, are you in there?"

Esme didn't recognize the voice and waited. Eventually, the feet went away, and she heard the bathroom door open and close. She gently set her feet down and glanced under the stall. The bathroom appeared empty. Her legs tingled from being in place for so long, so she bounced up and down in the stall to get the blood flowing again. Once she was sure she was alone, she pushed the door open.

Stepping out into the empty tiled room, Esme considered what she could do. She couldn't go to class, and she was going to be in trouble if she didn't. Becky was already struggling and Esme's defiance would only hurt her cousin more. She moved to the mirror and peered at her hair. From the front, it looked almost normal, but when she turned her head slightly to the left, she could see the missing chunk of hair. Becky was sure to ask what happened, however, Esme had no excuse for the damage. She couldn't tell her the truth.

Fishing around in her bag, she found a hair tie and did her best to gather the rest of her hair into a ponytail to hide to shorn section. Shifting her head left to right, she assessed her attempt at disguising the missing patch.

"That looks better," a voice behind her said, and Esme jolted at the sound.

She whipped around to see a girl about her age leaning against the far wall. She instinctively touched her hair and frowned. Had the girl been there the whole time? She glanced down at the girl's feet and saw the same worn sneakers she'd seen from under the stall door.

"Who are you?" Esme asked, not recognizing the girl from her class. Was she new?

"Martina, but you can call me Marty. I just started here today. The teacher, uh, what's her name, told me to come find you and see if you were alright."

"Ms. Norris," Esme replied, staring at the short, red-haired girl.

"Yeah, her. Ms. Norris. You are Esme, right?"

Esme nodded, not having had this long of a conversation with any other kid in the school. She shifted her bag over her shoulder and squinted at Marty. Would this girl turn on her like the others did? Sometimes, one or a few of the other girls would pretend to be nice to her, then, when she started to let her guard down, they'd attack.

Marty cleared her throat and stood up straight. "I don't bite, ya know."

Esme didn't know. She watched Marty with a mixture of intrigue and fear. "No one likes me here."

"Oh. Well, I'm not from here, so don't worry. They probably won't like me either," Marty replied and rubbed her freckled, snub nose.

On that, she was right, Esme considered. Marty was new like her. Newer even. Esme had been there for months, and Marty only started that day. Esme glanced in the mirror again at her hair and decided it was as good as it was going to be. "I guess we have to get back to class."

Marty nodded and grinned. "I guess so. Can't get in trouble on my first day, can I?"

"They're going to laugh at me," Esme replied, fear twisting her gut.

"So what. They're stupid. Don't worry, I'll go into the class with you."

The two girls headed to the classroom, pausing at the door. Esme looked at Marty, who nodded with encouragement. Esme pulled the door open, Marty on her heels. Snickers started in the room as soon as they entered, and the teacher immediately shushed the children.

She stared at Esme. "Glad you decided to join us, Esme. Please take your seat."

Terror washed over Esme as she saw her desk in the far back row of the room. She'd need to walk past all the other kids to get there. She felt a gentle hand on her shoulder and glanced behind her to see Marty smiling at her. Esme's mouth wobbled as she smiled back at her new friend, and she began the long trek to her seat.

The children made faces, and a few used their fingers to pretend they were snipping their hair. Esme kept her eyes forward, motivated by the fact she wasn't alone this time. By the time she made it to her seat and sat down, her breath was coming in short, ragged waves.

Marty sat beside her in an empty seat and shrugged at Esme, her mouth making the words, "See? Not so bad."

They focused on the teacher, and Esme felt like she just might be able to make it through the day. Marty stayed by her side the rest of the school session and on the bus ride home. Esme got off the bus and hoped the other kids wouldn't be mean to Marty once she got off. Something told her Marty could hold her own.

When Becky got home, she checked on Aunt Darla, who was like a zombie in front of the television set. Then, she set to making dinner for the three of them. Esme stepped in to help, chopping a salad while Becky made macaroni and cheese. They worked in silence when Esme forgot about her hair and pulled the hair tie out because it was hurting her head. She heard Becky gasp and jerked her head toward her cousin.

"Esme! What happened to your hair? Did someone do that to you at school today?" Becky asked, her fingers gently touching the shorn area.

Esme froze, not sure what to say. If she told the truth, Becky would have to get involved and go to the school. Esme didn't want that. If she lied, she needed to come up with a believable story on the spot. She shook her head, putting the hair tie back into her hair.

"No, my hair got caught in one of the badminton nets during gym. It got so tangled, they had to cut it to get me free," Esme replied, the lie coming too easily.

Becky watched her, her eyes filled with concern. "Oh, honey, I'm so sorry. Let's look at it after dinner, and I'll see if there is something I can do to fix it. Why didn't they contact me about that when it happened?"

Esme didn't want Becky calling the school, so she quickly shifted the conversation. "It's okay. I told them not to. It's nothing, it will grow back. Besides, I made a new friend today!"

Becky appeared like she didn't want to let the situation drop, but gave Esme a pained smile. "That's good. What's their name?"

"Her name is Marty, and she's super nice. She just started at school today. We sat by each other in class and rode the bus home together."

Becky nodded, stirring the mac and cheese mindlessly. She seemed pleased that Esme had made a new friend, but something behind her eyes said she was still worried. "I'm happy to hear that. Maybe you can invite her over for a slumber party one day."

Esme grinned at that idea. She'd never had, or been invited to, a sleepover. "Thanks, Becky! I can't wait to ask her. I bet she'll be excited to come over."

That night as she lay in bed, imagining all the things she and Marty could do, she saw Uncle Ray come to her door. He watched her from the doorway, his eyes sad.

He'd never done that before, or even registered her presence since he'd died. He was always standing by Aunt Darla like a guardian. Esme stared at him, trying to understand why he was there at her room. He shook his head, his eyes saying something his mouth couldn't.

Something she needed to know

Chapter Seven

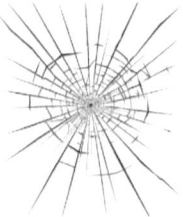

Marty and Esme became inseparable, and Esme finally felt like school wasn't some sort of cosmic punishment. The other kids paid them no mind, and Esme was relieved to see they didn't torment Marty like they had her when she arrived as the new kid. Then again, Marty was brash and fearless. Esme assumed this was why the other children steered clear.

They only had one class together as the school had them changing subjects and thus classrooms all day. They were in Ms. Norris's art class, and Marty was happy to sit in the back, doodling sketches of cats. Esme, on the other hand, was afraid to draw because adults always seemed to read into her artwork. Ms. Norris gave her prompts and ideas to trigger her imagination, but at the end of each class, all Esme could show for the time were spirals and shapes. Ms. Norris eventually gave up and let Esme do as she wished.

One day, a few months later, as Esme was leaving the class-room to go to lunch, fumbling with her sketchbook, a large, meaty girl named Sara came up and knocked Esme's books out of her hand. Sara had been the previously picked-on kid until Esme arrived and made sure she never fell back into that role again. This meant even with the other kids moving on from messing with Esme, Sara made sure to keep at it. To stay off the bottom.

Esme crouched to gather her belongings when Sara used her knee to push Esme to the floor. The other kids laughed until a teacher poked his head out into the hall to see what the commotion was about. Sara quickly ducked down the hall as if she'd never been there, and the other children disbursed.

The teacher glanced at Esme. "Are you alright?"

She nodded, casting her eyes down to give away the truth. If she said anything, it would only get worse. She shoved her books and papers into her backpack and rose. The teacher eyed her, then disappeared back into his class.

"That Sara needs her clock cleaned," a voice to Esme's left said.

She glanced over to see Marty standing right beside her. Esme hadn't noticed her friend come up. How long had she been there? Esme peered down the hall, but the bully was nowhere to be seen. "I wish she'd leave me alone. What have I ever done to her?"

Marty shrugged. "Maybe that's the problem. You haven't done anything, so she thinks you never will."

Esme considered she probably wouldn't and sighed. "Let's just go to lunch. You want to eat in the quad?"

The quad was a large open space between buildings the children were allowed to go on their lunch break instead of the cafeteria. Esme liked it because she could find somewhere away from the others to eat in peace. Marty bobbed her head, and they went outside. The weather was overcast as a light drizzle fell, so they were some of the only children out there. They tucked up under a tree and opened their lunch sacks. Marty always had better food than Esme, but Esme never complained. Becky was doing her best with what little she had.

Marty handed Esme a cookie and leaned against the tree. "You really should set Sara straight. She'll keep picking on you if you don't."

Esme chewed the cookie and shook her head. "I'm not like you, Marty. She scares me."

"Like me how?"

"I don't know. You don't seem scared of anything or anyone. That's why no one messes with you like they do with me," Esme explained.

Marty tapped her head, her red hair falling over one eye. "Yeah, I guess so. You need to stop being afraid of them, though. They are nothing."

They sure felt like something to Esme. She switched the subject, asking Marty if she wanted to have a sleepover at some point. Marty didn't answer at first, and when she did, it surprised Esme.

"My parents won't let me."

Esme waited for something further to explain why, but Marty focused on her sandwich in a way that let Esme know the conversation was over. Still, she wanted to know why Marty's parents wouldn't let her come over.

"Is it because of me?" she asked, her voice barely above a whisper.

"You? Why would it be because of you? No, they're just weird." Marty answered with a grin. "Aren't your parents weird?"

Now it was Esme's turn to clam up. She picked at the crust of her bread and shrugged. "I don't have parents. They died when I was little."

"Oh. I'm sorry, I didn't mean to bring it up," Marty replied softly. She reached out and touched Esme's hand.

"You didn't know."

Something about this information made Marty's demeanor change, and she finished her lunch quickly. A few minutes before the bell rang, she stood up and paced back and forth. Esme was confused by this change in her friend, and she frowned up at Marty.

"Are you okay?"

Marty paused her back and forth and placed her hand on her hips, her freckled chin in the air in anger. "You know, they shouldn't treat you like that with all you went through."

"Who?" Esme asked, glancing around as if someone was making Marty antsy.

"The other kids. Sara. They should be nice to you since your parents are dead. Instead, they make your life worse."

"It's okay. They don't know any better," Esme lied. Of course, they knew better, but it was easier to keep her head down and take it. To ignore the taunts.

"Yes, they do!" Marty yelled, shocking Esme into silence.

Marty was always outspoken, but now she seemed agitated. The bell rang for them to go back to class, and Esme gathered her things, thrown off by Marty's shift. She got up and stared at her friend, clutching her backpack to her chest.

"Are you mad at me, Marty?"

Marty whipped around, her eyes bristling with pent-up energy. "At you? No, Esme, you are my best friend. I'm mad at them for being so mean to you. They need to pay."

Best friend. No one had ever called Esme that, and the words warmed a small part of her heart. Her shoulders relaxed. "You're my best friend too."

Marty smiled, her body becoming less tense. "Come on, we'd better get to class before the sick the dogs on us."

Esme frowned. "Dogs?"

"It's just an expression, Esme. You know, like before they come after us."

The girls walked to the building and headed their separate ways as they went to their respective classes. Esme paused and watched Marty head down the hall, walking with confidence and an air of challenging anyone to mess with her. Her best friend. Esme smiled and felt her step was lighter. Things were looking up.

At the end of the school day, Esme searched for Marty outside to walk to the bus together, but didn't see her friend anywhere. Fear gripped her as she saw Sara cutting through the crowd toward her with a smirk on her face. Praying Marty would show up first, Esme gripped her bag in her hands and peered around. Where was she?

"Oh, look. It's the freakshow," she heard Sara say as a few kids around them laughed nervously. Esme ignored the taunt and shifted toward the buses, hoping to get there before Sara got to her. The buses were parked along the side of the road with their doors open as students loaded on.

Marty was nowhere to be seen, and Esme wondered if she'd gotten on the bus already. She hurried in the direction of her bus, keeping her focus on the open door. Sara didn't ride their bus, so once Esme made it through the doors, she was safe. At least for the moment.

All of a sudden, she felt something yank her back, and she tumbled to the ground, skinning her knee on the sidewalk. Sara had grabbed the strap of her backpack and spun her around, letting go as Esme lost her balance. Esme winced as blood pooled up on her skin and gazed up into Sara's red and angry face.

"Sara, leave me alone," she pleaded.

"What did you just say to me?" Sara spat, leaning over Esme with her fists balled up, ready to strike. Whatever anger was inside that girl, it had more to do than with just Esme.

"She said to leave her alone!" a familiar voice screamed, and Esme saw Marty running for Sara full speed. She struck the startled girl full force, sending her flying into the street. Sara was bigger, but Marty had rage on her side.

Esme jumped up, and Sara landed in the middle of the road, her mouth hanging open on a shocked O. Esme glanced at Marty, who was standing with her arms crossed, a smug look of satisfaction on her face. Esme looked back at Sara, who was struggling to her feet, tears in her eyes. Her legs were scraped up, and she seemed discombobulated.

A scream erupted near them, and all eyes darted to where it came from. A young girl watching the events unfold, had spied something the rest of them hadn't seen yet, her hand shaking as she pointed up the road. As if pulled by an unseen force, all of the children followed her trembling hand and saw it before it happened.

A truck coming down the road, its driver focused on the buses, was headed straight for Sara in the road. The truck couldn't stop in time before mowing her down, throwing her body several feet into the air. Sara's body was tossed up like a ragdoll and came down hard, the sound of bones crunching upon impact. The girl lay lifeless as the driver rushed out of the vehicle with his hands in the air in horror.

Esme froze in terror, then turned to Marty, who was no longer standing there. One of the boys from Esme's math class faced her, his eyes hard and confused.

"Esme, what did you do?"

She shook her head, disoriented. "I didn't. I..."

He pointed at the street toward Sara's form. "You pushed her in front of that truck. I saw you do it."

Esme's world began to spin, and she scanned desperately for Marty. However, it was only her standing there. "It wasn't me, it was Marty."

"Who is Marty?"

Chapter Eight

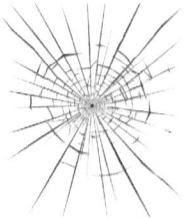

The following twenty-four hours were a blur. The police came to the school and interviewed all the children present on the scene, including Esme. She insisted Marty pushed Sara into the street to protect Esme from the attack by the larger girl. Not wanting to get Marty into trouble, she told the authorities Marty was only acting in Esme's defense. Becky was called to the school in lieu of Aunt Darla, who, although Esme's legal guardian, was practically an invalid.

Becky burst through the gym doors where they were interviewing the children and placed herself between the police and her niece, her face contorted with rage.

"Just what the hell do you think you are doing talking to Esme without an adult present? She is a minor for Christ's Sake!" she yelled at the teacher and uniformed officers.

"Who are you exactly?" one of the police asked cooly, eyeing Becky's tense figure.

"Who I *am* exactly is Esme's cousin and guardian," Becky spat, her eyes blazing.

"Legally?" the same officer replied with a sneer. Clearly, the school had informed him otherwise.

Becky's face turned red, and she clenched her fists at her side. "Regardless of the paperwork, I raise her, and you are interviewing her without a parent or lawyer present, so I recommend you wipe that shit-eating smirk off your fat, fucking face."

Esme's eyes grew wide as she'd never seen this side of Becky. The police officer also shut his mouth and made notes in his notepad, and refused to meet her gaze.

Becky took Esme's hand. "Come with me."

"She can't leave," another officer said. "We won't ask her any more questions without you preseentand you are free to get her legal counsel, but she is required to stay here until we are finished with our questioning."

"For what? Is she being charged for something?" Becky asked, grasping Esme's hand tight enough to hurt.

The authorities glanced between themselves, then one nodded. "Ma'am, again, she can't leave."

"Is. She. Being. Charged?" Becky repeated, her voice tight and controlled.

"At this time, we are looking at charges," the first officer replied, whispering as if he now wanted to protect the child from Becky's wrath.

"For what?"

"Ma'am, this may not be the best time or place to discuss this," he answered, not blinking.

"FOR WHAT?" Becky yelled.

The officer shrugged. "She was seen pushing another child into the road, who was then struck and killed by a truck. Manslaughter at a minimum."

Becky's mouth dropped open, and she let go of Esme's hand. She barely glanced at her niece before she set her mouth, then focused back on the police. "Then, I request a lawyer before you speak to her again."

The officers again looked at each other, and one cleared his throat. "Are you requesting a public defender?"

Becky nodded, deflated. She had no money for an attorney. Esme stood stock still, wishing to disappear. She shook her head and whispered, "It wasn't me, Becky. I swear. It was Marty."

Becky peered down at her and hissed, "Don't say anything else, Esme."

Esme felt shame rush up her body and settle in her cheeks. Becky was angry at her. She hung her head and didn't make eye contact. Where had Marty gone? Why was she letting Esme take the fall for something she did?

They were escorted to a classroom and told to stay there. A police officer was stationed outside the door to make sure they didn't try to sneak out. After a couple of hours of waiting, a thick woman in a suit at least a size too small came in, carrying a satchel.

"Ms. Collins? I'm Public Defender Marsha Bannon. I have been assigned to Esme's case. We need to go over a few things. I understand you aren't her legal guardian, but are here to represent your mother who is?"

"Yes, my mother is unable to be here. I have power of attorney for my mother. I'm sorry, her case? Is Esme officially being charged?" Becky inquired, her voice shaking.

Marsha pulled out a stack of papers and glanced at them. "Yes, I'm afraid so. All witnesses said Esme pushed Sara Dockery into the street after they were observed fighting on the sidewalk near the buses."

Esme heard her voice before she registered it was her own. "It was Marty! We weren't fighting. Sara threw me on the ground, then Marty pushed Sara to stop her. She didn't know a truck was coming!"

"Who is this Marty? Last name?" the public defender asked, jotting down notes.

Esme froze. She didn't know Marty's last name. How could she not know Marty's last name? They were best friends. Becky stared at her, waiting for her to reply. Esme wrung her hands in her lap, trying to think if she ever heard the teachers say Marty's last name. She hadn't, and the more she thought about it, she never remembered the teachers even calling on Marty for anything. Her friend always sat next to her in the one class they had together and drew in her notebook.

Seeing she wasn't getting anywhere, Marsha cleared her throat. "I'll ask the school about this child. However, at this time, witnesses say the altercation was only between Sara and Esme. Including the bus driver. This is what the police are considering in pressing charges. Let me go and chat with the school and see what else information I can gather."

Another hour passed before the public defender came back, and Esme was tired and hungry. Becky seemed to be detached, staring out the window at nothing. Esme glanced at her cousin, and panic set in when she saw Uncle Ray standing behind Becky. He had his hands on his daughter's shoulder and stared at Esme with a disapproving look. She began to tremble uncontrollably and sob, a vision of her hands on Sara's chest as she shoved the larger girl into the road.

She pushed Sara.

Screams erupted from her as she fell to the floor in an apparent seizure. The officer ran into the room, confused. Becky was on her feet, calling for help as Esme flailed on the tiled floor.

The last thing Esme remembered was the officer leaning over her and trying to hold her body still as Becky hollered over and over that Esme was dying. Then the world went black, and Esme slipped into delirium.

In her catatonic state, Esme saw Marty. Her friend was standing in the middle of an empty room. She seemed bigger, more scary than Esme remembered. She tried to run to Marty, to beg her to tell the truth about what happened, but her feet wouldn't budge. In fact, when she looked down, her whole body was wrapped in barbed wire, and she couldn't move.

Looking back up, she pleaded with Marty to help her, but Marty simply shook her head, her face stern. Then her eyes grew wide and black, her mouth opening into a silent scream. Esme mimicked the scream and thrashed in her bonds, the wire tearing into her skin. When she glanced back at Marty, her friend was no longer alone. Gogo and Tall Man stood with Marty, the three of them laughing at Esme in her struggles. Their cruelty cut more than the barbed wire wrapped around her body.

Esme never felt so betrayed and allowed the barbs to eat into her flesh, knowing she deserved it. Marty, Gogo, and Tall Man walked to a door, which had appeared in the far side of the room, and opened it. Esme begged them not to leave her behind, but they acted as if they couldn't hear her. One by one, they passed through the door without looking back at the young girl crying on the ground.

Esme felt the floor open beneath her and suck her down into a dark abyss. She fell for what seemed like years, her arms trapped to her side so she couldn't reach out to stop the perpetual fall. She hit the ground full force, her body breaking into a million little pieces.

The breath sucked back into her body, and Esme returned to her body with a jerk, her eyes flying open. Bright lights surround her, but her arms were still pinned to her sides. She tried to kick herself free, however, she was immobile.

"Calm down, Esme. You won't be able to move and will only hurt yourself," a calm but sterile voice told her.

She strained her eyes to find the source of the voice and landed on a shape in white. As her eyes focused in, she saw it was a woman in a long white coat. "Where am I?" she asked, her voice trembling.

"You were attacking yourself and were transferred here for your own safety," the woman replied.

"Here?"

"You are in a special ward of the hospital. Do you remember what happened?"

Esme shook her head. "Marty? Sara?"

The woman picked up a chart, peering at it, then nodded. "Do you remember what you did to your friend Sara at school?"

"She's not my friend. She picked on me all the time. Why can't I move?"

"You were clawing at yourself. You have cuts all over your arms and legs from your fingernails. We didn't want you to hurt yourself anymore, so we have you tethered to the bed for your own safety. I'm Dr. Martin."

Esme glanced at her arms and saw bloody scratches all over them. Not barbed wire, her own nails. She met the doctor's eyes and understood she was in deep trouble. Flashes of Marty, Gogo, and Tall Man laughing at her came back, and she began to cry, the tears stinging her cheeks. She'd injured them, too.

Dr. Martin rose and came over to Esme, her face kind but concerned. "You are alright, Esme. We will take care of you. I am stepping out to let your cousin know you are awake. Then we need to run some tests."

Esme knew those tests wouldn't help her. They would prove she was losing her mind, something she'd suspected since she remembered pushing Sara into the street. Not Marty's hands but her own. Not Marty's anger, Esme's. She recalled meeting Marty in the bathroom the first time and now could see only herself in the mirror reflection of the tiled area. She put herself in class and turned her head to see only an empty seat beside her. Eating alone at lunch. Riding the bus home by herself.

Marty was her.

Chapter Nine

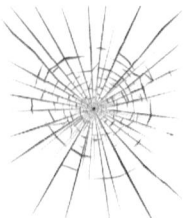

The next few weeks felt like months, and Esme was unsure of anything around her. Memories and reality fragmented into one another, and she didn't know when she was awake or asleep and dreaming. The two blurred into one long dream state. Often, she was told to swallow pills from a little paper cup, and she was too young and confused to know to refuse. Not that she could have, they would have simply injected her to keep her complacent.

Becky seemed to float in and out, but when Esme would focus in, Becky would be gone. If she'd ever been there, it was hard to tell. The one thing she knew for sure was she wasn't home, and the place she existed day in and out served to be nothing more than a holding place. No one was cruel, but no one was comfortable either. Faces blended into one another until it appeared like one being in white coming and going.

Egg-shaped faces, moving mouths. Blinkless eyes and a hum that never stopped.

Even in the dark of night, it hummed.

The first moment Esme felt she could comprehend time again, she was sitting in front of a barred window, staring out. She didn't know how she got there or how long she'd been sitting in that place, but her hands were twisted in her pale blue fabric gown. Like a hospital gown from television shows. She rubbed her fingers over the stiff material and frowned. Had she put it on? She couldn't remember doing so. She also couldn't remember eating or using the bathroom at any point. Time had become nonexistent.

Her eyes scanned around the space, and everything seemed sterile. Grayish whites, dingy blues, pale yellows, which seemed more like aging or stains than intentional coloring. She was in a large room of some sort. A few tables and chairs, a couch that looked like it was made out of plastic. A television droned across the room, too quiet to make out what was being said, too loud to be peaceful. No one was watching it. In fact, no one seemed to be in the room except Esme.

She realized the chair she was in had wheels and wondered if she could no longer walk. Setting her feet on the cold, white tile, she tested her strength. Her legs shook and felt unnatural, but she was able to rise out of the chair. She braced herself on the windowsill and turned around. The room was empty. Esme wondered if she was the last person alive.

Taking a few halting steps toward the plastic couch, Esme stared down at her legs, not recognizing them as her own. Her knobby knees stuck out from the medical gown, and her feet splayed weirdly out. Yet they kept moving forward, and she trusted them to get her to where she was going. Where that was, she didn't know.

Finally, arriving at the weird molded seating area, she shifted onto the shape and sat down, the coolness of the plastic cutting through the fabric around her. Everything here felt cold. The couch had a little give, and she ran her fingers across the strange sticky surface.

She tried to focus on the television, but the people on there seemed alien, their mouths moving but not saying anything she understood. No matter how hard she tried to focus in, their words were gibberish. Had she been abducted and taken to another world?

A door cracked open across the room, or was it on the television screen? Esme couldn't tell. A tall woman came through the door, her mouth twisting in a weird shape. *A smile,* Esme's brain told her, all the while doubting it was true. Esme watched the woman approach with a sense of fear and distrust.

"Hello, Esme. I'm Dr. Martin. We spoke when you first arrived here at the hospital, do you remember?"

Even if Esme had, her mouth didn't work, so she simply stared at the doctor, whom she didn't recognize.

Dr. Martin leaned forward, touching Esme's hand. "It's okay, you were on some pretty powerful medications. We have reduced them now that you seem to have calmed down. We didn't want you hurting yourself anymore. Do you know where you are?"

Esme shook her head. Not home. Dr. Martin nodded as she glanced around the too brightly lit room. "You have been admitted here to Bellamy Hospital for evaluation. You are safe here, and we are simply here to help. The courts have requested a full status on your mental health for the trial."

Esme tried to speak, but her lips stuck together like someone had smeared paste and pieces of paper over them. Then she realized she had nothing to say, anyway. She wasn't even sure if she was there or if Dr. Martin was real. If even she herself was real. Nothing made sense in her brain.

Dr. Martin made a hand motion in the air, and a man in a grayish-white uniform with stained armpits entered the room. Dr. Martin smiled at him, then back at Esme.

"This is Mario. He is going to show you your room and take you for a walk outside. Would you like that, Esme?"

Hearing a complete stranger say her name with such familiarity made Esme want to scream, but her mouth refused the motion, so she only whimpered. Mario stared down at her, his large, brown eyes holding no animosity.

He put his hand out to her, but Esme simply gazed at it, not understanding the intent. Dr. Martin touched Mario's elbow and shook her head. "She's probably still out of it from the medications. It will take a while for it to lower enough in her system for her to comprehend basic intent. Why don't you grab her wheelchair by the window and guide her to the room? Then you can take her on a tour of the grounds. Fresh air might do some good to clear the medication fog."

"Yes, Dr. Martin. Do you want me to bring her back to her room once we are done, or for dinner?"

"Back to her room. Dinner in the cafeteria may be too much stimulation for Esme right now. Have a tray brought to her room." Dr Martin focused her attention on Esme. "You are safe here. We want what's best for you to help you get better. If you need anything, don't hesitate to ask. I can't promise we can get it for you, but we will do what we can."

Esme could register what they were saying, but as soon as her brain caught it, it flitted away like a butterfly, leaving her unsure of what was said or how to respond. She stared back at the television, the dancing bucket on the screen making more sense to her than the doctor.

Mario brought her chair over and touched Esme's arm to help her move into it. She let him assist her into the chair, sure she was still also sitting on the couch facing the television. However, when she looked back, she wasn't there.

She didn't remember the tour outside or seeing her room. The next moment she recalled was being wheeled back into a space Mario said was hers and staring at a tray of food on a small metal table. Mario guided her to the table and gestured to the food.

"Eat something, little one."

Esme gazed up at him, her head rolling around her shoulders. He sighed and sat on the edge of her bed. "Here, let me help."

He scooped up a spoonful of... something and moved it toward her mouth, touching her lips with the edge of the spoon. "You need to eat. Otherwise, they'll need to put you on a feeding tube. You don't want that. Here, like this."

He opened his mouth and motioned the spoon toward it. As if on instinct, Esme mimicked the gesture, and he slipped the spoon to her mouth, using his finger to close her mouth with her chin. The substance in her mouth felt strange, but she swallowed it. Mario smiled.

"That's it. You're coming around. Once the medicine wears off, you'll feel like yourself again." He gave her a few more bites, then Esme stopped swallowing and let the goop slide back out of her mouth onto her clothes.

Mario nodded. "Good enough for today. Let's get you into bed. Hopefully, tomorrow they can remove your catheter and you'll start feeling like yourself again."

Catheter. Esme didn't know that word. Mario shifted her from the chair to the bed and plumped up her pillow. Something about him felt like her earliest memories of her father. Of being carried around. Mario moved toward the door and paused. "Sleep tight, Esme. If you need one of us, there is a button beside your bed. Press it, and we will come check on you. Get some rest. You'll feel better in the morning."

None of that made sense, and Esme stared at the wall, her ability to stay conscious slipping in and out. Mario wasn't real. Dr. Martin wasn't real. She wasn't real. She'd died when her mother did, and all of this was some strange dream.

She closed her eyes and went back to the womb, back to before she began in this world. That was the place she felt safe and wanted. Home. The waves of amniotic fluid swayed her back and forth, back and forth. Esme relaxed and let the motion take her away from everything.

A sudden gush of cold air washed over Esme, and she was forced out of her cocoon, being thrust back into the world. Except there were no hands to catch her, and she slammed hard against a wall. No, not the wall, against the floor.

She flailed, her arms and feet smacking against metal. Forcing her eyes to open, she saw she was hitting the underside of the bed and the end table. Her mouth still wouldn't move to cry out for help, and the table knocked over, clanging loudly on the floor. Esme curled herself into a ball, trying to go back into her hiding place.

In an instant, Mario and another person in the same uniform rushed into the room and lifted her off the floor, placing her back into the bed. Their hands ran over her body, checking for injury from the fall. Seeing there was none, Mario went to flip on the light switch, his face worried.

When he did, Esme saw something else in the room and began to scream, her lungs forcing her mouth to do what it couldn't until then. She squeezed her eyes shut and thrashed uncontrollably in the bed, attempting to get away from what she saw. Mario quickly pulled straps out from under the bed and wrapped them over Esme, pinning her in place.

"Call Dr. Martin," he yelled to the other person, who bolted out of the room.

Mario sat on the edge of the bed, stroking Esme's hair. "It's okay, Esme. You're alright. You just had a bad dream and fell out of bed. I'm sorry I had to use the straps. I don't want you to injure yourself. I'll remove them as soon as Dr. Martin comes to check on you and says I can. Are you hurting anywhere from falling when you had the nightmare?"

Except Esme knew she hadn't had a bad dream. She'd been awake when he turned on the light and exposed the darkest corners of the room. The places hidden in the dark. No dream, no nightmare, could be as scary as what she saw hiding there, waiting for her to be alone again. Waiting patiently for Esme to be vulnerable and unable to call out for help.

It was hiding, ready to pounce.

Esme couldn't take her eyes off the large, scary form hovering in the shadows, despite the fact seeing it made Esme want to retreat inside herself and never come out again. It held her in a trance, crawling into her brain.

A tall, thin creature with peeling skin, stringy red hair, long arms, and pointed, dirty fingernails. Its face marked with razor-sharp teeth held in a cruel smile, and piercing green eyes that bore into Esme's soul. Telling the young girl it was only a matter of time until she would be all alone and helpless.

Easy prey.

Chapter Ten

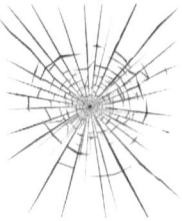

The subsequent years passed like paint peeling in an abandoned building. Esme spent her days in her room, in therapy, and wandering the halls like a lost soul searching for relief. In lieu of charges for Sara's death, Esme was ordered to spend the rest of her youth in the hospital. Institution, really. A place to lock away the mentally ill. *Crazies* is what most of the staff called them behind their backs. Not all, though. Not Mario. Which made Esme even more convinced he wasn't real.

He wasn't real, but the creature that followed her, hiding in corners in every room Esme was in, *was* real. That much she knew. The creature mocked her, its long fingers pointing out her every flaw, scratching her body in the night. In order to compartmentalize its reality, Esme assigned it a gender and a name. It became a *her*, and *she* became Lamia, a name of a child-eating, serpentine creature with removable eyes, Esme read about in one of her aunt's mythology books. Esme wasn't exactly sure why, but it mattered, and putting a name to it controlled the being's power over her.

Aunt Darla never visited, but Becky did often. She came every week and never treated Esme like a freak. Not like Lamia did. Sometimes when Becky would visit, they had to sit in the recreation room, as the staff called the large, dismal, white space. Lamia hovered over Becky, mocking her and eyeing Esme to see her reaction. Esme assumed Becky couldn't see Lamia, so she never brought her up.

Becky did seem to see Mario, though, which threw Esme off. They would chat and smile at each other as Lamia drooled on Becky's shoulder. Mario seemed to hang around more when Becky visited. Esme didn't like that. She didn't want her imaginary person to interact with her real people, so she'd scream and throw things at Mario to make him leave, upsetting Becky, who'd never seen that side of her cousin. Esme had always been quiet. A little odd, but never violent. This often ended with Esme back in her room, Lamia laughing in the corner.

"I hate you," Esme whispered at the ugly creature, despising its strange head turns after one such event.

Lamia shifted her large, sinewy head back and forth and hissed, "I hate you," right back at Esme in her own crackly voice. That was the only way the creature spoke out loud, mimicking Esme.

Esme squeezed her eyes shut and shook her head. "Stop tormenting me."

"Tormenting," Lamia repeated and cackled.

Esme could feel the creature's breath on her body and smelled rotting fish emanating from Lamia's flesh. She knew if she said anything else, Lamia would hiss it back at her, so she kept her mouth shut and turned away. She hated Mario for making her miss her weekly visit with Becky. Why was he always there? He was messing with her head, pretending he could interact with her cousin.

Esme shoved herself under the soft comforter Becky had bought her a year prior and lay down, her back to Lamia. She could still feel the creature watching her and tried to ignore the eyes boring into her back.

"Stop it. I want to go to sleep," she muttered, instantly regretting it.

"Go to sleep," Lamia whispered, her dry, crackled voice drawing out the word *sleep* like a snake.

That was how it went every day. Lamia following and repeating Esme like a demented shadow. Lamia was her punishment for killing Sara, Esme believed. Her penance for being a terrible little girl. She deserved her fate and the stinking beast who was as much a part of her reality as her own feet were. Esme accepted that and the fact she would never leave the confines of the hospital until she was an adult at the soonest. This was her home, and Lamia was her shackle.

As the years passed on, Becky came less, eventually only coming once a month. Mario had also disappeared from Esme's life, and like Tall Man, Marty, and Gogo, Esme figured he'd served his purpose in her alternate reality and had moved on. Somewhere in another plane of existence, they all lived, laughing about what a fool she'd been to let them in. Mocking her and conspiring against her.

As she neared her eighteenth birthday, Becky hadn't come to visit for months, so Esme decided that, like her mother,

her father, Aunt Darla, and Uncle Ray, Becky had washed her hands of Esme and gone on with her life. Esme had improved in her therapy, so the doctors said, and was soon to become an adult. Becky didn't need her anymore. Esme was nobody's. Well, except Lamia and that bitch continued to torment the teenager relentlessly. Esme never told her doctors about Lamia; she knew they wouldn't believe her. Even if they did, they might use it as an excuse to never let her leave.

After about four months of no visits, Esme was surprised when she was called to the rec room for a visitor. She didn't know anyone except her family, and they were done with her. To her surprise, a plump woman was sitting with her back to the door Esme was entering from. Esme frowned, knowing there must be some mistake. The woman must be there for someone else. She turned to the nameless orderly walking her in, but the worker pointed at the woman in the chair.

Esme moved closer, her feet shuffling toward the table. The woman rotated in her chair, her mouth in a strained smile. Esme froze. Becky? The woman in the chair looked a little like her cousin, but also like Uncle Ray. She had also put on a lot of weight. The woman's smile faltered.

"Esme, it's so good to see you," she whispered, her voice not backing up her words. She seemed nothing but unhappy to see Esme. "Come sit and let me see you."

Esme did as she was told, staring at the new Becky. Becky's hands ran over her belly, and Esme froze. Becky wasn't plump; she was pregnant. Very pregnant. Following her gaze, Becky sighed.

"Hey, hon, I need to tell you some things. I'm sorry I haven't come to see you in a while. I, uh. Well, as you can see, I am having a baby. In a couple of months. I was pregnant the last time I came to see you, but I wasn't showing yet. I had some bleeding, and the doctor thought it was best if I didn't overextend myself and put me on bed rest for a few months. I really am sorry I haven't come to see you in a while."

Esme sat silent, trying to process what was happening. How could Becky be pregnant? She stared at her own hands on the table, hearing Lamia's jagged, yellow toenails scratching on the floor behind her. She shook her head. "How?"

Becky frowned, clearly trying to understand if she needed to explain sex to Esme, then leaned forward. "Honey, I met someone and we are starting a family. We aren't married yet, but will be after the baby is born. This was a ll a little unexpected, but we are excited about meeting this baby and starting a family."

Lamia cackled, spittle flying through her stained teeth. Esme waved her hand back to silence the creature. She narrowed her eyes at the not-quite-right Becky. "So, why are you here now?"

Becky recoiled and stared at Esme, her eyes filling with tears. "Esme, you are my family. I love you. I wanted you to know. I need to tell you something else, too. I feel it's only fair to be honest."

"To be honest," Lamia sibilated, mimicking someone other than Esme for the first time.

Esme jerked her eyes to the hideous beast and whispered, "Shut up."

Lamia wasn't fazed, but Becky was, bursting into tears, thinking Esme was speaking to her. "I shouldn't have come here. I need to go. Esme, I don't know why you hate me so much. I have been here for you, even when everyone told me not to. I... never mind. I'm sorry. I hope you know how much I love you."

Becky rose, her hands shaking as she pushed the chair in. She stared at Esme, then, seeing she wasn't getting a response, nodded to the orderly she was ready to leave. The orderly opened the door and smiled at Becky, the one who got to leave.

As Becky passed Esme, the thin girl's hand shot out and gripped Becky's wrist. Becky paused and stared down at her niece. Esme's eyes rose to meet hers, and the hardness in them made Becky stiffen up.

"Who is the father, Becky?" Esme asked, Lamia's voice coming out of hers.

Becky glanced away, the secret between them weighing like a ton of bricks. She cleared her throat. "Do you remember the man who used to work here? Mario? He really liked you, Esme. Cared about you. It was tough on him to leave, but considering the circumstances, he and the hospital felt it was best to not cause any issues."

Esme's eyes formed slits as she peered at Becky. "Mario? I don't understand."

Becky's face flushed as she looked away, her mouth quivering. "Esme, he's the baby's father. We... we hit it off and started seeing each other a little over a year ago. That's why he quit. He felt it was a conflict of interest to work with you and date me. Then with the baby..."

The room began spinning, and Esme didn't even realize she was on top of Becky, punching her over and over until she heard Becky's screams. Orderlies rushed in and pulled the teen girl off her cousin, who was bleeding and sobbing on the floor. Becky scrambled away, being helped to her feet by one of the orderlies, as the other worker secured Esme's arms to her sides. Becky wiped tears and blood off her face as she stared in horror at the girl she'd been trying to protect for so many years. She wrapped her hands around her stomach and backed away.

Esme spat toward her, Lamia's voice belting from her chest. "He's not real! I made him up! He's not real!"

With that, Becky fled the room and out of Esme's young life. She stopped for a brief second at the door, her eyes showing the hurt and shock she was feeling. She ducked her head and ran.

Lamia leaned back and roared with laughter as Esme fell to the floor, the sedative injected into her arm taking hold. Esme stared at the creature and accepted her fate as the world around her went dark.

It was just the two of them now.

Chapter Eleven

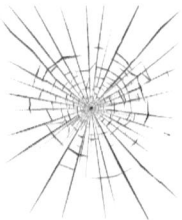

"Do you understand, Esme?"

Esme's eyes jerked up to meet the doctor's. No longer Dr. Martin, who'd moved on a few years prior. Dr. Hubach. He was soft-spoken and too patient. It irritated her sometimes. He was young; they usually were. No one stayed there long enough to grow old. Most of them came fresh out of school and cut their teeth on the *crazies*, then went off to open their own practice or go somewhere less chaotic. They always said they cared about the residents, but they always left, even so.

Always.

The doctor waited patiently for Esme to respond, but the words stuck in her throat. How was she supposed to understand anything? She'd come there as a child and was now being asked to understand the adult world she was unfamiliar with. She shook her head.

Dr Hubach sighed. "I'll try to explain it a little simpler. When you were sent here as a child, it was because you had a mental break, which caused you to harm someone. Rather than send you to prison, you were sent here for care and observation. We always thought your family would take you back in when you hit adulthood, but, um, well, in light of what happened between you and your cousin, you don't have family to go back to at this time. The state won't let you stay here as an adult, and I don't think prison is the right decision for someone in your..."

He trailed off, but she knew what he meant. Her *condition*. Sure, she'd made "great strides" in her treatment, and they didn't believe she was a threat to herself or anyone else. *Anymore.* She'd learned to tell them what they wanted to hear and denied the presence of any unseen guests. Even as Lamia breathed down her neck at that very moment. Esme gently touched the back of her neck, expecting it to be wet and slimy, but it was soft and dry.

"Where will I go, then?" she asked, genuinely concerned they would simply put her out on the street to fend for herself.

"Well, we have options. We can transfer you to a state-run facility for adults, but those are rough and overcrowded. We are privately funded for trials, and your care was covered by a program for at-risk youth. The other facility isn't, and, unfortunately, I don't think you would thrive there. We do have programs for adults here, but you don't currently qualify for them."

Esme frowned, not wanting to be sent to another place. "What are the other options?"

Dr. Hubach leaned forward, his thin metal-framed glasses slipping down on his pointy nose. "Without a family or other sponsorship, we really only have one other choice. It would be a big change for you."

"Okay?" Esme questioned, Lamia's hair brushing her cheek as the creature leaned down closer to not be ignored. Esme went to brush it away, realizing that might look crazy to Dr. Hubach, so she redirected and faked a cough using her raised hand to cover her mouth.

He leaned back in his chair and stared out the window before answering. Esme noted he looked about Becky's age. Becky, who by now would have a child and probably married to Mario. Becky, who never came back to see Esme. Mario, who apparently was real, after all.

"There are homes, called halfway houses. Halfway because they help you bridge the difference between being in here and out there. I'm not sure you are ready for such a drastic change of environment, but our hands are tied. They will help you get a job, enroll in school, things like that. They also offer daily therapy group sessions."

"Oh."

It was all she could think to say. She thought she'd be locked up the rest of her life. The idea of living halfway into the world was not unwelcome, but also terrifying. Dr. Hubach smiled, but his eyes didn't seem included in the motion. They seemed worried.

"They have trained staff who live there, and you will continue your individual therapy out there, as well. The home we are considering has five other women like you. Getting back on their feet," he explained.

"Women," Lamia hissed, then laughed dryly.

Esme ignored her now constant companion, but also found the word strange to her ears. Woman. She was still a girl, but not in the eyes of the state. She'd hit eighteen years old, a legal adult, it was time to move on and move out. Discarded like always.

Always.

"Do you understand? Is this something you think you could do, Esme?" Dr Hubach asked, making it clear the question was merely politeness. She didn't have a choice.

She nodded, wrapping the hem of her gown around her fingers so tightly, the tips of her fingers turned purple. Dr. Huback wrote on a chart and rubbed his upper lip with his pointer finger, distracted. He only did that when he wasn't telling the whole truth. Esme had learned to recognize all the doctors tells, the things they did when they were hiding something. It was how she saw through the rhetoric to what they were actually thinking and not saying.

She sat up straight and did her best to look on board and clear. "When would I go?"

He looked surprised and glanced back at the charity. "Oh, uh, let me look into that. Soon. We would need to arrange your space and make sure they can fit you in. Maybe a week or so. I'll let you know as soon as I hear something."

Esme rose and cleared her throat. "I need to go. It's dinner time."

Dr Huback gazed at the clock on the wall and nodded, his mind elsewhere. "So it is. Head on to the cafeteria. I will see you in a few days. I won't be here for a couple of days. I have some time off."

Esme narrowed her eyes. Time off. He got to leave into a world she didn't know anymore. Not as an adult. He met her eyes and smiled. "I'll let you know as soon as we get your new accommodations arranged."

He said it like she was going on vacation. Travel agent for the criminally insane, she thought to herself. Esme brushed past Lamia and went to the door. She knocked twice to let the orderly know she was ready to leave. The generic, fit in any mold, orderly opened the door and escorted her to the cafeteria. No one was like Mario. He'd been kind and got to know the patients. So kind, she thought she'd made him up. Apparently, she hadn't, and he'd run off with Becky. Replaced Esme with a better version... a new baby.

She went into the cafeteria and grabbed an empty tray, heading into the line for food. Everyone shuffled like their feet were unable to lift more than a half inch off the ground. Mostly it was the medication. People came in fighting and full of electricity, and eventually, they moved like the rest of them. Including Esme.

How would she ever survive on the outside?

After mindlessly eating her dinner, Esme went to her room, hoping sleep would come. It didn't, and she paced restlessly in her room, thinking about what the doctor told her. She hated it at the hospital, but she knew it. It was familiar. She had routines and expectations. She knew people, at least enough to know who to avoid. On the outside, she had none of that. No guidance, no protections. She might lose whatever sanity she'd reclaimed inside these walls.

Lamia mocked her the whole night, calling her a baby and crazy. Esme didn't doubt the creature, but at the same time, didn't have time to argue with her. Esme had her mind on the future, something she hadn't needed to think about in years. Something she thought would be taken care of for her.

"Shhh," she ordered the smelly monster in the corner. "I need to think."

"Need to think," Lamia screeched back, making Esme cover her ears.

Would Lamia go with her? The serpent with peeling skin didn't show up until Esme was in the hospital. Maybe she was trapped there. As if Lamia understood Esme's thoughts, she shrank, her green eyes paling to a jade color. The creature's mouth twisted in worry, and she leaned close to Esme for some type of reassurance.

Esme frowned, not understanding the sudden change in Lamia's demeanor. Realizing what Lamia was requiring, Esme replied, "I don't want to take you with me."

"Take you with me," Lamia expressed, the words not quite right but the intent crystal clear. She tormented Esme, but couldn't live without her. They were intertwined, and Lamia's existence depended on Esme.

For a moment, Esme felt sorry for Lamia, then shook her head. "Stop it, I need to think."

Lamia fell silent, and when Esme glanced back, the creature was gone. All of a sudden, Esme panicked. Lamia was always there. "Lamia? Where are you?"

The room was quiet, and Esme shivered. If Lamia wasn't with her, then she would be in the world completely alone. She hated Lamia, despised her constant presence, but she'd become used to Lamia being there. Esme sat on the edge of her bed and punched the mattress over and over. Rage filled her, but she bit back the steam to not draw attention ot herself. Any variation of her behaviour was noted and could cause her suffering. Treatments to reset her brain.

Esme needed to stay calm.

She started pacing again, trying to imagine the halfway house. Would she have a room of her own or be forced to share with someone else? What kind of job would they make her get? Would they watch her every move? How would she eat? Shower? Sleep? Breathe?

Her thoughts were becoming chaotic and panicked. She pinched her arm to stop the spiral and tried to take deep breaths to settle her racing heart. She didn't want to go. She was scared of feeling like she was falling endlessly. Terrified of not having a safety net like she did at the hospital. She didn't know what was real out there. *Who* was real.

She crawled into a corner of her room and wrapped her arms around her legs, burying her face in her knees. Fighting back tears, Esme felt reality slipping away from her. The floor began to open up, and she knew she was about to be swallowed whole into the vast chasm forming, eating everything in its way.

"Lamia, I'll take you with me," she whispered, knowing she had no choice and didn't want to end up totally alone in the world.. Only silence greeted her. She peered up and saw her room shifting into a channel to hell. She gripped the wall to keep from being sucked in. She needed something to anchor her in place before she was dragged under and could only think of one thing.

One being.

"Lamia! You can go with me!" she screamed out into the void.

Something long and stringy tickled her head from above. Esme gazed up to see Lamia leaning over her, her wide mouth and glistening yellow teeth stretched in joy as she repeated Esme.

"Go with me."

Chapter Twelve

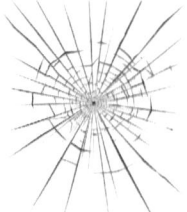

T he room was small and drab, smelling of floor cleaner and dust. Esme set her bag on the twin bed and glanced around the space. Everything was decorated in beige tones and appeared to be thrift store throwaways. For some reason, that seemed fitting, even welcoming. The woman who'd shown Esme to her room stood in the doorway, her face tired and disinterested as she droned out the information Esme needed to settle in.

"Dinner's at five thirty. If you miss it, there's always sandwich makings in the cabinet and fridge. Everyone takes turns cooking during the week. We have group sessions at eight in the morning and eight at night. You need to attend at least one, but are welcome to go to both. You can't leave without notifying someone unless it's for work, and we need your schedule each week. If your work schedule changes, let someone know. You share a bathroom, so be respectful of how long you are in there. There's a shower schedule on the wall outside the bathroom door. If you need to take a shower outside of the schedule, just make sure no one else is slotted for that time. This is your room, however, the door must always be unlocked in case of emergency," the woman said, clearly having repeated the monologue many times before.

Never mind that Esme didn't have a job yet and had never cooked a meal a day in her life. Hopefully, they'd be able to teach her that and other life basics. She nodded and waited for the woman to leave, not sure what to say. The woman watched her, then sighed.

"I'm Lisa, the evening supervisor. Sheena comes in at six in the morning. We are both certified therapists. Our floaters are Cathy and Elizabeth, though Cathy only comes in to cover when one of us is out, so you won't see her very often. Elizabeth is regular part-time as she is in school to become a therapist. She is here when one of us is to shadow and covers breaks. It's all women here, so don't get any ideas about sneaking guys into your room. That will get you tossed out on the street real fast. Do you understand?"

"Understand," Lamia whispered, taking her place in the corner, her presence smaller than usual.

"Yes, Ma'am," Esme answered.

"Alright, I'll let you get settled in. Call me Lisa, not ma'am. I expect you for dinner and tonight's session. This is required on your first night here. You need to meet the other women and get to know your way around."

Women. The word still felt foreign, and Esme didn't see herself that way. In her mind, she was still thirteen years old, still needing to be taken care of by an adult. Yet, here she was at eighteen and expected to be an adult in the world.

After Lisa left, Esme plopped on the bed and covered her eyes, hiding from her new reality. Even Lamia was oddly quiet in the room. Esme wanted to cry to let the pressure out, but the tears wouldn't come. She couldn't think of the last time she'd cried. Instead, her eyes ached and felt hot, too big for their sockets.

She hadn't realized she'd dozed off when a light knock at the door startled her awake. She jerked up and stared at the open doorway, confused for a moment as to where she was. A woman who appeared to be in her early thirties stood there, her hand on her hip.

She gestured with her head. "Come on, dinner's ready. They expect the new women to be there to meet everyone. I'll show you the way to the dining room."

Esme blinked a few times, trying to get her bearings. She nodded and stood up, smoothing the provided clothes she was wearing. Sweat pants and a t-shirt. Since she'd outgrown any clothes she'd been wearing when she was admitted to the hospital years before, they'd scrounged up some clothes for her to take back into the world. A bag of generic items to wear.

"I'm coming," Esme replied, her voice sounding foreign and robotic.

"Follow me. I'm Allison, by the way. I'm one of the residents here."

Esme moved toward the door, still foggy from her unexpected nap. "I'm Esme."

"Esme? That's a very pretty name. Where's it from?" Allison asked as she led the way down the narrow hall to the top of the stairs.

"My parents?"

At that, Allison laughed. "I meant, like, what nationality is it?"

Esme had no clue. "I don't know. It's just what my parents named me."

Allison didn't respond as they headed down the stairs. Esme peered around, noting the decor in the whole house was dull. It was a two-story house with six bedrooms. Well, four bedrooms and two converted spaces made into bedrooms, so each woman had her own space. Six women total. The house was full at the time, but it sounded like women came and went all the time. She wondered where the therapists slept, or maybe they didn't, since they rotated shifts.

Expecting a cafeteria, Esme was surprised when they came into an actual dining room with one large table and everybody crammed around it. All eyes were on Esme as she found an empty seat and sat down. The women were mostly quite a bit older than her, but one girl at the end appeared to be in her twenties. Esme dropped her eyes, feeling the pressure of being new.

Lisa, the supervisor, cleared her throat and put her hands in front of her. "Let's say grace."

The women all closed their eyes and put their hands in front of them. Esme frowned, not understanding when Allison nudged her, motioning for Esme to clasp her hands. Esme did and peered through slitted eyes at the other women as Lisa droned some sort of prayer. The women all murmured to themselves in repetition.

Esme caught sight of Lamia in the corner, mimicking the women, her long fingers wrapped together as her yellowed nails reached up her arms. For some reason, this made Esme laugh, but she caught it in her throat and grunted instead. Lisa stared at her, and Esme fell silent.

As soon as grace was over, plates of food were handed around, and Esme took a small amount of each to be polite. She wasn't hungry and dreaded what came next. Conversation. Questions she didn't want to answer. Luckily, one of the women liked to take and took over the room with her ramblings about work and someone named Stacey, whom she didn't like.

After the woman had gone on for about ten minutes, Lisa stopped her, making the woman scowl. "Thank you for sharing, Donna, however, we have a new guest here, who we need to get to know. Esme, would you like to introduce yourself?"

Donna shot daggers with her eyes at Esme for being interrupted, even though Esme didn't want any part of introducing herself to begin with. She fiddled with her fork as she thought of what to say. She cleared her throat nervously. "I'm Esme. I'm eighteen and, uh..."

She didn't know what else to tell them. She was Esme, she was eighteen, and she didn't think they'd want to know about Lamia or her past, so she fell silent. The other women waited for more. When they saw they weren't getting it, they glanced at Lisa.

Lisa smiled. "I see. What do you like to do, Esme? Read? Sing, Draw?"

Esme didn't do any of those things. Now that she thought about it, pretty much all she did at the hospital was watch television and wander the halls. They'd had books and art supplies, but she wasn't interested in them. She was in her head most of the time, with TV as a distraction to give her brain a break. Everything she did outside of that was required as part of her therapy there. Journaling, drawing, things like that were assignments, not for pleasure. However, now she felt stupid to say that, so she blurted out the first thing she could think of that came to mind.

"I like to write."

"What do you write?" the younger woman at the other end of the table asked, her curiosity piqued.

Esme's brain scrambled for an answer, then remembered one of the other patients at the hospital insisting they all listen to his stupid poems. "Poetry."

She'd never written a single poem in her life. Not even for therapy.

"Lovely," Lisa replied. "We have a sharing session each week on Friday nights. Each of the women shares their personal talents, and we would love for you to read some of your poems for us."

Lamia began to cackle in the corner, and Esme's face flamed as she realized she was caught in her lie. All eyes were on her, so she bobbed her head. "Okay."

They went back to eating dinner. Esme picked at her food, listening to everyone talk. Mostly about work and people they didn't like at their jobs. Lisa constantly redirected the conversation to prevent any one person from hogging the time or spiraling into a rant. She tried a few times to draw Esme into the conversation, but Esme had nothing to say. Maybe once she had a job, she'd feel like being part of the group. Right now, she simply wanted to crawl into a hole and hide.

After dinner, Allison asked Esme to help her take the dishes to the kitchen while the other ladies put away the food. Esme grabbed plates and followed her into the fairly large kitchen. Allison began washing the dishes in the sink and handing them one by one for Esme to dry.

"Grab that towel over there and wipe these off. You can stack them next to the sink. Lisa likes to put them away because she doesn't like how we do it." Allison rolled her eyes and laughed.

Esme wanted to ask Allison why she was there, but knew that would open the conversation to why she was there as well, which she wasn't ready for. So she dried the dishes silently. Allison began to hum to herself, which reminded Esme of Becky. Becky would always hum or sing while she was doing chores.

It was comforting.

Distracted, Esme didn't realize Allison was handing her a plate, and it slipped from Allison's hand, shattering on the floor. The sound startled Allison, and she stopped humming, her eyes large. Her face contorted, and her pleasant demeanor shifted as her face became twisted and red.

"You stupid bitch!" she screamed at Esme. "Now look what you have done."

Esme froze in terror, not understanding what was happening. Lamia grew larger in the corner, her green eyes flashing in anger. Lisa ran into the room to see what the commotion was about, and a quick scan of the situation set her into full gear. She rushed over and put herself between the two women, facing Allison.

"Allison, count to ten. Remember where you are," she coaxed, her voice firm, but guiding.

Allison stared past Lisa at Esme, her eyes filled with rage. Lisa motioned for Esme to take a step back. Esme did, but bumped into a counter behind her. Her hands were shaking, and her face felt flushed. Lamia came up beside her, her stringy hair hanging over Esme's shoulder. Lisa kept her eyes on Allison, but called out to another woman, the younger one from the end of the table.

"Ginny, will you show Esme the way back to her room? I'm sure she'd like to get some rest before our session tonight. Esme, Ginny will show you the way back upstairs."

Ginny came over and touched Esme's arm, her eyes locked on the stare down between Lisa and Allison. "Come with me."

Esme followed her out as Lisa focused on Allison, her voice calm but firm. All Esme heard as she left the kitchen was Lisa saying, "Not your father."

Ginny walked in silence to Esme's room and turned to face her once they got there. "Sorry about that. Allison has a real bad temper. My room is just down the hall if you need to talk. I work in the morning but am home by six every night on the days I work."

Esme stepped into her room and attempted to smile at Ginny, but her mouth felt odd, made of plastic. Ginny gave her a small wave and walked down the hall out of sight. Esme went to her bed, her legs feeling like rubber, shaking like crazy. She sat on the edge of the bed, her mind reeling with what just happened. Taking deep breaths to settle her heart, she couldn't get Allison's angry face out of her mind. What happened in the kitchen? One moment, Allison was joking and chatting; the next, she was out for blood.

Lamia took her place in the corner, agitated and scratching her nails against the wall repeatedly. The sound hurt Esme's ears and made her anxious.

She glanced at Lamia. "Please stop."

Lamia didn't.

Esme watched the door, expecting someone to appear. No one did, and Lamia's ragged breaths set her on edge. Ginny called the place home, but this was no home. Home was somewhere safe. This was unfamiliar, scary. She wanted to go back to the hospital.

Esme felt something she hadn't in a very long time and welcomed the pain in. The squeezing in her chest and the flood of emotion forcing its way out from deep inside her, released out of the cavern she'd forced it into years ago to keep herself safe and in control.

Esme burst into tears.

Chapter Thirteen

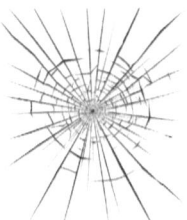

E sme didn't see Allison for over a week after the incident. She suspected Allison was avoiding her after flipping out in the kitchen. They had the option to eat separately, and the only required group activity was the morning and evening group sessions. Esme always went to the evening one, so Allison must have been going to the morning one. Lisa seemed on edge and pulled Esme aside one afternoon.

"I don't usually get involved, but I think we need to have you and Allison sit down with us to talk things out. It's unhealthy to keep avoiding the issue and will only grow the longer it is left to stew."

"Us?" Esme asked, confused.

"When we have a situation, we pair up to address it. Elizabeth has offered to sit in as another neutral party. We need to talk about what happened between you and Allison."

Esme felt the hair raise on her arms. What Lisa was saying sounded like an accusation and reminded Esme of the day with Sara. Her defenses went on high alert. "I didn't do anything! She went at me!"

Lisa's eyes darted around uncomfortably. "I know, Esme, however, we are not allowed to choose sides, so to speak. We are supposed to address any issues in a balanced and neutral way. We'll simply listen and guide if the conversation between you two gets out of hand."

Esme felt seeds of anger bloom and kept her face still to show any emotion. "I didn't do anything wrong, but if I have to do this to be here, then fine."

Lisa's face relaxed a little, and she forced a smile. "You'll see, this will bring peace between you two."

Esme seriously doubted it and turned to go upstairs without saying anything else. Lisa didn't try to stop her or hold it against Esme for leaving so abruptly. She was probably used to it.

Esme went to her room and opened a journal. Since she'd told everyone she was a writer, she was attempting to do just that. She scribbled a few lines of poetry, realizing they were terrible, and flipped the page to a fresh sheet. She began to sketch like she had in Ruth's office, drumming up memories from being a child and loving to draw. Her mind zoned out as her hands flew across the paper. When she looked at what she'd drawn, she held her breath.

Tall Man was her father, Lamia her mother, Gogo was Becky, and Marty was standing behind a window of a house, her mouth opened in a scream. Esme scanned the picture. She wasn't in it. A couple of large blobs in the living room of the house Marty

90

was in, she assumed were Aunt Darla and Uncle Ray, but she couldn't say for sure. Her cousin John wasn't there, but he never really was to begin with.

Esme slammed the book shut and gazed at Lamia in the corner. The creature had seemed less strong since the run-in with Allison, and this made Esme feel vulnerable. Lamia hissed at her from her spot, her yellow teeth bared. Esme hissed back and lay on her bed. It was almost dinner time, and she wasn't sure she wanted to deal with everyone. The forced conversations wore her out.

She had an appointment the following morning with a career specialist. Career. More like the worst job she could probably find. She had no skills and no experience. Everyone in the house worked jobs from cleaning hotel rooms to fast food. They were required to work a job for three months before they were allowed to have unapproved time outside of the house. So whatever they could get for freedom.

A sharp rap came at the door, and Esme frowned, not expecting anyone. "Come in?"

Lisa opened the door and stuck her head in with a smile. "Hey, you have a few minutes to have a mini session before dinner? Elizabeth is here, and Allison is willing to meet with us."

Esme assumed she didn't have a choice in the matter and sat up. "I guess so. Where?"

"We can sit in the garden room. It's private and calming," Lisa replied.

The garden room was an enclosed back porch filled with light and houseplants they all took turns taking care of as part of their household chores. Esme liked it, but someone was usually already in there, so she rarely went on her own. However, when it was her turn to water the plants, she found the space peaceful.

"Okay. I'll be down there in a minute."

Lisa left, and Esme took deep breaths to center herself. Something Dr. Hubach taught her at the hospital. Lamia did as well. Esme climbed off the bed and shoved her journal under her mattress. She didn't understand what her picture meant, but she didn't want anyone else seeing it and jumping to the wrong conclusions.

The garden room was dimly lit and cozy, as the sun had gone down, when she arrived. Buttons, the house cat, was curled up in one of the chairs, leaving only the one across from Allison available. Esme considered moving the cat, but she looked so content sleeping there, Esme couldn't do it. She sat in the other chair, trying to not meet Allison's eyes. She noticed Lamia didn't come into the room, instead hanging outside the doorway, peering in.

Strange.

"Okay, please remember this needs to be constructive. Elizabeth and I are here only as mediators. We need to respect our purpose in the house, and that is to heal. Allison, you agreed to this session, so is there anything you'd like to say to Esme?" Lisa asked, her voice calm and clear.

"Sorry," Allison muttered, not looking up.

"Thank you for that, Allison. However, I think it might be helpful for you to tell Esme why you are sorry and what triggered your episode that night in the kitchen," Elizabeth encouraged.

Allison shifted uncomfortably in her seat and shook her head like she was getting bugs out of her ears. She replied, "The plate."

"What about the plate?" Lisa pushed.

Esme frowned, completely lost on what was happening. "Because I dropped the plate? I'm sorry. It was only an accident."

Allison's eyes jerked up, blazing with anger. "Bad girls drop plates."

Esme glanced at Lisa for clarity. Lisa touched Allison on the hand gently. "No, people drop plates, Allison. It happens to everyone. They get slippery, right? From water and soap. It's no one's fault."

Allison's mouth twisted oddly, and a low voice came out of her, not her usual perky voice. Gruff and masculine. "I ought ta whip you, child. You did that on purpose to make me mad. You little brat."

Elizabeth shook her head at Lisa, this wasn't going as planned. Lisa nodded, they needed to de-escalate the situation before it progressed any more. Lisa glanced at Esme, gesturing with her head for Esme to leave the space. Esme was confused and began to feel like she could leave her body, her hands shaking uncontrollably.

What was happening?

Lisa stared at her firmly. "Esme, why don't you go ahead and go to dinner. We can pick this up later."

Esme rose and took a step back. This motion caught Allison's attention, and she bolted out of her chair, lunging full force at Esme. Esme ducked, but not in time as Allison clawed her across the cheek. Esme cried out, and Lamia howled in rage outside the room. Jumping out of their chairs, Lisa and Elizabeth grabbed Allison and held her back.

Esme was stunned as they struggled to control the woman. Lisa grabbed a handheld radio and spoke into it, her eyes meeting Esme's. Was that fear Esme saw in them? She inched toward the door and stepped through the threshold just as Allison broke free from Lisa and Elizabeth.

"I'll kill your Goddamn cat!" she bellowed, rushing toward Buttons, who was woken up by the ruckus. Allison reached for the confused feline, and Esme panicked, knowing Allison was going to hurt the cat.

Lamia stepped forward, through Esme, and struck Allison with a watering can, which had previously been on a hook by the door, knocking her out. Buttons bolted out of the room in terror. Esme stared at Lamia, realizing the watering can was now in her own hands. Elizabeth began to cry as Lisa ran over to Allison, crumpled in a heap on the ground.

Lisa stared up at Esme. "It's okay. She's breathing, just unconscious. Esme, I need you to leave and go back to your room. We'll handle this. Don't say anything to anyone on the way to your room. We'll have your dinner brought to you, so you have time to be alone and recover from this situation."

Esme felt shame, like when she was told she'd pushed Sara into the street. She shook her head. "She was going to hurt the kitty."

Lisa nodded. "Honey, I know. I need you to go to your room and not speak to anyone. Can you do that? Elizabeth, can you go with her? I have help coming."

Elizabeth hiccuped as she wiped tears off her face and walked over to Esme. "Yes."

She led the way out, and Esme followed, fear gripping every ounce of her being. They were going to send her back to the mental hospital for what she did.

"She was going to hurt the kitty," she kept whispering, more to herself.

Elizabeth didn't reply, her shoulders hunched as she ascended the stairs. When they got to Esme's room, Elizabeth paused and met her eyes.

"I'll bring you dinner." She turned to leave, then paused, only one word escaping her lips. "Buttons."

As if that opened the floodgate, Elizabeth began to sob again and hustled down the hall. Esme stumbled to her bed and lay on it, staring at the ceiling. She'd messed up this time. She wasn't healing; she was a monster. The image of Allison lying on the floor unconscious came to mind, and she shuddered.

She *was* a monster.

Lamia began to screech in the corner, clawing at her arms. Skin peeled and oozed as Esme watched in shock. Lamia never hurt herself. Esme felt distressed and sat up.

"Stop," she whispered to the creature.

Lamia continued injuring herself, and Esme jumped out of bed. "Lamia! Stop!"

Lamia froze, her green eyes fixed on Esme. Something else was held in them. Not only cruelty and venom. Pain. A layer Esme had never seen before. Lamia genuinely seemed to be hurting. Esme stood frozen in confusion. The creature was evolving, it seemed.

Lamia dropped her long arms, her sharp nails scratching the wall on the way down. She hung her head as her thin flame-red hair fell over her face. A deep, long wail came out of her body.

"Going to hurt the kitty... Esme stopped Allison," she cried out, her face contorted in suffering.

It was the first time Lamia spoke words that weren't simply a repetition. She understood what happened.

So did Esme.

Chapter Fourteen

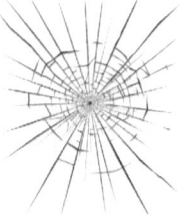

T he next morning, Esme stayed in her room, waiting for the inevitable. She was sure they were sending her back to the hospital and began to gather her things to be ready when they came to take her away. After a bit, Sheena came to the door and asked Esme to follow her downstairs.

"Do I need to bring my stuff with me?" Esme asked, hovering near the bed.

Sheena frowned, staring at the pile Esme had made of her belongings with confusion. "Your stuff? Oh, uh, no. Dr. Hubach is here to see you."

Dr. Hubach? Why would he be there at the home? She hadn't seen him since she left the hospital. All the residents' therapy was done in-house with daily sessions and weekly visits with an assigned therapist. So, Dr. Hubach being there was completely out of the blue. Or maybe not, considering Esme hit another resident of the home. Esme glanced at Lamia, who seemed agitated and on guard.

Were they staying at the halfway house after all?

Sheena waited for Esme at the door, and they walked down to the therapy room together. Sheena paused at the door as Esme stepped inside, then she left without another word. As promised, Dr. Hubach was in there and smiled at Esme as she came into the room.

"Are you settling in okay, Esme?" he asked, his glasses glinting from the overhead light. He seemed out of place in the different environment. Less intimidating.

Esme shrugged. She'd really just gotten there, and things were anything but okay. "I guess so."

"Lisa told me what happened with Allison, so I want to apologize for your experience with that. This is not your fault. Lisa explained how Allison has been become increasingly detached and aggressive lately. How she went after the house cat, um, sorry, I can't remember its name."

"Buttons and it is a *she*," Esme replied flatly.

"Buttons, right. They asked me if I'd come see you since you haven't developed a relationship with the assigned therapist yet. They thought you might need to see a familiar face after what happened. Would you like to sit down and talk for a bit?"

Esme didn't want to, but understood the question was more rhetorical than anything. They were doing a check-in to make sure she was stable. She sat down in one of the plush chairs across from Dr. Hubach. Only a coffee table held the space between them. "It's weird seeing you here."

"I'm sure it is. First, let me tell you that Allison has been sent back to full care and will no longer be in the home," Dr. Hubach explained.

Full care meant the hospital. Esme tipped her head, attempting to read between the lines. "Am I being sent back there, too?"

Dr. Hubach looked genuinely surprised. "No. What happened was out of your control. Yes, you shouldn't have hit Allison, but considering she threatened to kill and then went after the cat, I imagine most of us would have done the same thing in the moment. I do want to talk with you about your reaction to what transpired last evening, though. Do you feel you were using logic when you took the watering can to stop Allison?"

That was the thing. Esme didn't remember grabbing the watering can and saw Lamia with it before Lamia passed through her to get to Allison. Then, the can was in Esme's hand, but she didn't put it there. However, she couldn't tell Dr. Hubach that. About Lamia.

"She was going to hurt the kitty," she repeated like she had told herself over and over the night before.

"Yes, it appears she was. Can you think of a better way you could have handled the situation?" Dr. Hubach asked, stroking his chin mindlessly with his fingers.

"No," Esme replied, not having any clue what else she could have done at that moment. Everything happened so fast, and Allison was out for blood. Lamia, who was standing off to the side, hunched, snickered, and hissed.

"Well, that's some real honesty. I appreciate you speaking your truth. Let's talk over some alternatives to handling the scenario, so next time you have better tools to deal with it."

"Next time?" Esme asked. Did he really think there would be a next time?

Dr. Hubach shook his head. "Theoretically. These tools can help in many different situations. So let's do some role play to see if we can de-escalate rather than attack, alright?"

Esme nodded, though she hated role play. "Okay."

They spent the next hour going over scenarios where someone was being aggressive and how to either calm them down or remove themself from the environment. They did talk about if the person became violent like Allison did, and what the best course of action would be. Even Dr. Hubach admitted, it depended on the situation.

After they were done with the role play, the doctor asked Esme some questions about her general well-being and encouraged her to keep a daily journal. She didn't tell him she already was, as she was afraid he'd ask to see it. After they said goodbye, Esme climbed the stairs to her room, exhausted from the session. They always did that to her. She flopped face-first on her bed and dozed off.

When she woke up, something about the room felt different. Larger. She peered around and realized Lamia was no longer with her in the small space. Had the creature come back from the therapy session with Dr. Hubach with Esme? She couldn't recall, but she did remember Lamia in the room with them, mocking Dr. Hubach.

Esme sat up and pushed her sweaty hair off of her face. Why would Lamia leave? She'd never done that before. Had Esme made some sort of breakthrough talking to Dr. Hubach? No. She could feel that wasn't it. Something darker, heavier was at play. Everything was very off.

Esme felt the hair rise on her arms.

Esme headed down the stairs, searching every corner and room she passed, looking for Lamia. The creature was nowhere to be found. Esme went into the therapy room, but it too was empty. Esme was confused and more than a little scared. She wandered to the kitchen, where she saw Lisa and Sheena whispering as they prepared food.

They saw Esme and stopped.

"Are you alright?" Lisa asked. "Did you have a good session with Dr. Hubach?"

Esme shrugged. "Yeah. I lay down afterward and fell asleep."

Lisa squinted, trying to read Esme's face when Buttons ran through the room, stopping to purr and rub on Esme's shins. Esme bent down and scooped the kitty up, remembering how Lamia had crossed a level of understanding the night before. How she'd spoken a thought rather than repeating what she'd heard.

Is that why she left?

"Looks like you have a new friend," Lisa said with a smile. "You earned her trust."

Esme rubbed the cat's soft golden fur against her cheek. She set Buttons down and chewed her lip as she considered where Lamia could have gone. "I'm going to sit outside for a bit, if that's okay."

"Of course, honey. We'll let you know when food is ready. Don't forget there's a little library on the back porch if you want to read something," Lisa replied and got back to chopping vegetables.

Esme slipped out of the kitchen and headed for the back porch. She browsed the books in the wooden box and settled on "The Secret Garden", one she remembered from her childhood. She stepped off the porch into the backyard and found a bench to sit at under a large oak tree, enjoying the sun on her face. She tried to read, but her mind kept going back to Lamia and where she could possibly have gone.

Esme set the book down and closed her eyes, pointing her face toward the sun. The image of Alison screaming and running for Buttons kept coming to mind, and she couldn't shut it out. She had to admit, hitting Allison with the watering can had made her feel powerful, even though she didn't quite remember doing it. Not necessarily in a good way, but powerful all the same.

After the food was ready, Esme took a plate to her room, hoping Lamia would be there. She didn't like the creature, but she'd grown accustomed to her presence, and her being missing set off alarms in Esme's head. Her room was still empty, and Esme set her plate of food on the bedside table. She went to the corner where Lamia always stood and placed herself there, pressing her back to the wall as she took deep breaths in and out.

All of a sudden, an image of Allison in the hospital came to mind. She was cowering in a corner as a large shadow loomed over her. She had her hands in front of her face and was crying, pleading, though Esme couldn't understand her words. Allison was frantic, her eyes round with fear. Esme felt a strange sensation as if she was in the hospital room and reaching out for Allison. She jumped out of the corner, her heart racing.

Stumbling to her bed, she sat on the edge and stared at the corner. What just happened there? Her hands shook as she placed them in her lap and tried to understand the vision she'd had. It was as if she was there in the room with Allison, standing over her even as she was in her own room.

Should she tell someone? No, they wouldn't believe her. She pulled out her journal and began writing, careful to not say anything that could get her into trouble if it was found. After a few minutes, her heart settled, and she set the journal down. She scooted over to eat her food, trying to shut the image of Allison out. It was only stress from what happened the night before, she convinced herself. Nothing more.

A scratching sound came from the corner, and Esme turned to see Lamia standing there. Except with her back to Esme, which was unusual. The creature shifted from side to side repeatedly, dragging her nails along the wall as if she was anxious. Esme wasn't sure if she was relieved or disappointed Lamia was back.

"Lamia, where were you?"

Lamia turned her head slightly, so Esme could make out her profile, but didn't turn all the way around. Instead, she continued her strange dance in the corner, her breath ragged and excited. When the creature spoke, her voice was high-pitched and odd, her words well-formed.

"Not hurt kitty anymore."

Chapter Fifteen

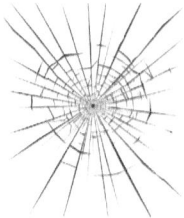

The dynamic in the house changed, and Esme felt everyone become more on guard. Especially around her. She overheard Lisa talking to Dr. Hubach on one of his visits around a week later. He came by to visit Esme again on an "unofficial" basis, which she found odd, but now everything was strange.

Esme wondered if they were considering sending her back to the hospital even though he'd assured her they weren't. Still, she felt like she was under a microscope. So after Dr. Hubach had her come to the therapy room to "chat" for a bit, she hung out in the hall, hiding in the shadows to listen to what they were saying in her absence.

Lisa went into the room, and Esme heard them talking in hushed tones. Esme swore she heard Lisa crying and inched closer to the door to hear better. She could see the edge of Lisa's shoulder and heard muffled sniffs. Esme could only make out Dr. Hubach's hands on the desk, but he was moving them expressively. She heard her name come up and Allison's, then more sniffing.

When Lisa's chair scraped against the floor as she moved it back to rise, Esme moved away from the door, but not before she heard the word "suicide" and Dr. Hubach consoling Lisa. Esme darted down the hall and waited near the kitchen. She saw Lisa leave the room, coming toward where she was standing. Esme came out of the shadows, acting like she was coming from the kitchen, and smiled at Lisa as she neared. Lisa definitely had been crying. About what?

"Hey, Lisa. Do you need help prepping dinner?" Esme asked, making her voice clear and chipper.

Lisa paused, seeming confused, then nodded. "Sure. I need to do a few things, but why don't you meet me in there in about fifteen minutes?"

"You got it. I'll go follow up on a couple of job leads in the meantime," Esme replied.

"That's good. Hey, Esme?"

"Yeah?'

Lisa stared at her like she wanted to say something, then shook her head. "I'll see you in the kitchen shortly."

Esme watched her, and Lisa turned down the hall to the staff room. She didn't say anything else, and Esme frowned. Lisa clearly wanted to tell her something. Something about Allison? Or maybe about Esme?

Esme went to the study room and sat at the desk with the phone. She called a few jobs she'd applied for and secured an interview as a waitress at a pizza place in town, walking distance from the home. Since the halfway house wasn't in the town

Becky lived in, or where Esme went to school, she felt safe in working such a public-facing job. Either way, she needed to show Lisa and Dr. Hubach she was moving forward and didn't need to go back to the hospital.

She headed to the kitchen, excited to tell Lisa about the interview. As she neared the kitchen, she could hear Lisa talking with Elizabeth and paused outside the door to listen. What they said made her blood run cold.

"They say she committed suicide," Lisa whispered.

"I don't understand. Allison was doing so well here. It's like something took her over," Elizabeth replied, her voice heavy with emotion. "I thought she was almost ready to go out on her own."

Lisa sighed, "I did too, but you know how this goes. Sometimes people self-sabotage out of fear."

"I guess so. But suicide? Did they say how Allison killed herself?"

"Dr. Hubach said she hung herself, but it was off. He said she was covered in long scratches like she'd been attacked by a cat or something."

Elizabeth gasped. "Buttons?"

"No, she never got to the cat that night, and she didn't have the scratches when she left here. I don't know. Maybe she did it to herself. She wasn't one who self-harmed normally, but she was under a lot of stress," Lisa suggested. "Anyway, we probably shouldn't talk about this here. Esme's coming to help with dinner."

They fell silent, and Esme waited a minute before entering the kitchen, her mind reeling. Allison committed suicide? Esme felt genuinely bad. Something about her had set Allison off; now she was dead. Her mind went back to Lamia saying about not hurting the kitty anymore, and the image she had of Allison crouched in the corner, crying with her hands up as if to protect herself.

Lamia hadn't left Esme's bedroom since showing back up, which Esme found strange, but she figured since she was working on getting a job, Lamia was starting to separate from her. Now she wasn't so sure. She made her face blank and went into the kitchen with a smile.

"Hey! I got an interview!" she stated proudly.

Lisa smiled, her eyes cloudy. "That's great news, Esme! Where at?"

"Mama Jo's Pizza. For a host position."

"Oh, that's wonderful. You'd be good at that. When's the interview?" Lisa asked, handing Esme a load of bread and a tub of margarine. "Butter these."

Esme took the items and sat at the table, opening the loaf. She took a butter knife and began spreading the bright yellow margarine across the slices. "This Wednesday at two."

Elizabeth slipped out of the kitchen without saying anything to them, leaving only Lisa and Esme in there. Lisa peered at Esme, the same expression she'd had before in the hall on her face.

"Esme, I need to tell you something. It's serious. Not sure exactly what I'm allowed to say to you all, but Allison won't be coming back," she said.

"Because she's back at the hospital?" Esme inquired, playing stupid.

Lisa appeared like she was struggling with her words, then nodded. "Something like that. Look, if you ever need to talk, please come find me. I don't want you to..." she trailed off.

Commit suicide? Esme set the butter knife down. "Thanks, Lisa. I will."

They finished prepping dinner, and Esme excused herself to take some time in her room before they ate. She climbed the stairs and slipped into her dark room, turning on the bedside lamp. Lamia was in the corner but seemed to be in a state of sleep or something of that nature. Esme cleared her throat.

"What did you do?" she asked.

Lamia didn't answer, but her eyes opened a slit. Drool dripped off her pointy, yellowed teeth as a creepy smile began to spread across her broad face. Her nails trailed down the wall almost playfully.

Esme felt a chill run down her spine, and the image of Allison at the hospital popped into her mind again. "Lamia, did you do something to Allison?"

Lamia nodded, her head going up and down in a slow but deliberate manner. She raised her arms in the air and brandished her long fingernails, dragging them down through the air. "Not hurt kitty anymore."

Esme took a step back and sat on the edge of the bed. How could Lamia have found Allison in the hospital? Then again, Esme never saw the creature before the hospital, and she was the one to bring Lamia with her to the house.

"Did you go to the hospital to see Allison?"

"Aaaaalllllliiiiisssssooooonnnnn," Lamia repeated with a hiss, drawing out the name in long syllables.

Now, Esme knew for sure Lamia had something to do with Allison's suicide. Allison's death. Anger filled her as she remembered Tall Man and her Uncle Ray's death. Like with her uncle, she couldn't say for sure her secret companion had anything to do with the death.

She also couldn't say they didn't.

Esme began to shake. Thinking about Allison, about Sara, about her Uncle Ray. Her parents. People around her died. She didn't want them to. More often, she just wanted to be left alone. Uncle Ray hadn't done anything to her, either. Not like Allison and Sara had.

Had he?

Flashes of memories came into her mind, and she saw Ray standing at her doorway, then sitting on her bed. His hands reaching.... NO! She shook away the memories and jumped up. Uncle Ray was nice to her, like a father. Yet, something in her kept screaming to think. Not *something*, the little girl she'd been.

Esme ran out of the room and hurried down the stairs. She needed to be somewhere else. She grabbed plates from the cupboard in the pantry and began setting the table to keep her mind busy. As the other women filtered into the room for dinner, Esme tried to fight the feeling of dissociation washing over her. She smiled and nodded a greeting as she sat in a chair, grasping the wooden handles in her hands to feel like she wasn't floating away.

Elizabeth and Lisa brought in the dinner and set it down, then took their seats. Esme remotely remembered hearing them say grace and putting food in her mouth, but the whole time she was attempting to bring herself back to that plane of existence.

As soon as dinner was done, she got up and left the room, afraid her inability to stay in her body was apparent. She went to the bathroom and locked the door, taking deep breaths. Staring in the mirror, she saw a wide-eyed girl with long, dark hair staring back at her. Part of her mind told her it was her, but the girl in the mirror was mocking her.

Esme turned away from the mirror, pressing her hands back against the cold ceramic sink. She was losing it. It wasn't the first time she'd dissociated, but it was one of the worst. She could feel the girl in the mirror's eyes boring into the back of her skull, but refused to turn around to face her. She pinched her arms to use the sensation to bring her back to herself and let her breathing steady. She wasn't dying. She wasn't *dying*. She *wasn't* dying. *She* wasn't dying. She wasn't dying.

The room became real again, and Esme rubbed her face, recognizing the sensation. She slowly rotated and looked at herself in the mirror, seeing only herself staring back. Not the other her. Splashing cold water on her face, Esme returned to herself. She dried her face and fixed her hair. She drew air deep into her lungs and smiled.

It was going to be alright.

Skipping the evening session, Esme went to her room to read and write in her journal. The light was still on from when she'd left for dinner before, and she eased the door open, peering into the space. Lamia was gone. Not like the time before, Esme knew in her soul.

This time, she hoped for good.

Chapter Sixteen

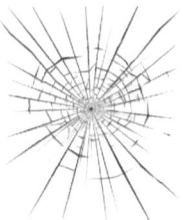

The next few months progressed quickly, with Esme getting hired at the pizza place. It was a hole in the wall, but they stayed busy. "Mama Jo" was Joanne Dickerson, and she was just that. Everyone's mother. She never had any children of her own, whether by choice or unable to, and she filled her maternal desires in nurturing pretty much everyone she came into contact with.

Including Esme.

Esme wasn't sure what to make of the fifty-something woman hurrying around the kitchen, filling in wherever necessary and being a little too cozy for Esme's comfort. If she hadn't seen everyone else interacting with Mama Jo, or "call me Jo, honey," Esme would have believed she was another figment of Esme's imagination. Jo was too *everything*. Too kind. Too hard working. Too funny. Too smart. Too *there*.

Over time, Esme let her guard down and let Jo in. It happened one night after the dinner rush, and Esme swore she saw Mario walk by the restaurant with a young child, a baby really, in his arms. The child was around a year old with a head full of dark curly hair. They were gone in a flash, and it might not have even been Mario, considering he didn't live in that town, but it sent Esme into a tailspin. She dropped a stack of cups she'd been carrying from the dishwasher, sending them scattering. They were the thick, see-through, bumpy, plastic red kind, so they didn't break, but still made Esme embarrassed and scrambling to recover both the cups and her senses.

"Don't sweat it, honey. That's why I buy this kind. Indestructible," Jo said as she picked one up and tapped it with her long red fingernail.

Even so, Esme felt her face flame and apologized in a series of incomprehensible mutters. By the time they'd gathered all the runaway cups and brought them back to the dishwasher, Esme was sure she was beet red and not from the exertion of chasing the cups.

Jo closed the dishwasher door and leaned against the counter, watching Esme. "Everything alright? I know it's a little embarrassing to drop stuff in front of everyone, but you seem like there's more to it than that."

Esme stared at the floor, not wanting to make eye contact. "Yes, ma'am."

Jo laughed heartily and stood up off the counter. "Ma'am? Woo, you sure know how to make a woman feel old. Here I was thinking I was fooling all you young ones into believing I was thirty-something, but you saw right through my charade, now didn't you?"

Esme couldn't help but glance at Jo, who gave her a quick wink. Despite attempting to keep everyone at a distance, Esme liked Jo. In a way, she had the elements Esme always imagined her own deceased mother to have. Open, caring, funny. Esme felt at home with Jo, and for that reason, she needed to stay away from her. People around her got hurt.

However, Jo was having none of that business. Her voice softened, and she closed the kitchen door, going out into the plating area. "You seemed mighty upset, Esme. Care to tell me what happened there? Did a customer say something mean to you?"

Esme shook her head. "No ma'-, I mean, Jo."

"Another employee?"

"No. It's nothing here. I just thought I saw someone I knew walk by out of the blue."

"Oh. Did you want to go say hello?" Jo asked, trying to get Esme to open up.

"No!"

"I see. That kind of person you know. I have a few of those myself. Anytime you feel uncomfortable, you're welcome to step away and take a break. Let me know and I'll cover for you, alright?"

Esme felt the warmth coming off Jo and let her guard down a bit. "Thanks, Jo."

Jo laughed and tipped her head. "You aren't one much for conversation, are you? I'd say if you ever need to talk, but I can see that ain't gonna happen anytime soon."

Esme's eyes darted around the kitchen, looking for something to focus on. Jo observed her for a moment, then grabbed a bucket of loose silverware. "Why don't you wrap these in napkins, and I'll handle waitressing for a bit. Give you a chance to get your thoughts together."

Esme wasn't sure if Jo was being kind or dismissive, but when she looked at the woman, her eyes were nothing but sincere. "Are you sure? I can go back out there."

Jo chuckled. "I don't mind. Honestly, I hate wrapping the silverware, so you're doing me a huge favor."

Esme smiled, feeling her muscles relax. She wanted to tell Jo how much her thoughtfulness meant, how she reminded Esme of the mother she never had. How working at the pizza place made Esme feel like she belonged for the first time in her life. Instead, she squeaked out, "Okay."

Over the next few months, Jo continued to reach out to Esme. Never in a pressuring way. She always joked and kept things light, allowing Esme to slowly warm up to her. During the restaurant's holiday party, Jo gave Esme a cruiser bicycle with a daisy basket as a gift.

"I see you walking to work all the time. Thought this might make your travels a little lighter," Jo said with her characteristic wink.

Esme was beside herself. No one had treated her in such a caring way. Not since Becky. Even thinking about Becky hurt Esme's heart, and she wished she could go back and handle things differently when Becky told her she was pregnant. She couldn't; things were the way they were.

She rang the little metal bell on the handlebars and smiled. "Thanks, Jo. It's so pretty."

Jo touched her shoulder with a grin. "Hey, I think someone else would like to talk to you."

Esme frowned. Who wanted to talk to her? She glanced at where Jo was gesturing with her head and saw Pete, one of the new cooks, staring at her and blushing. Panic set in, and she turned away, pretending to look over the bike. He was cute, but she'd never had anyone interested in her before.

Jo sighed with exasperation. "Kids these days. Pete, come check out Esme's new bike."

Esme wanted to scream and run away. Instead, she forced herself to smile and look at the approaching guy. It wasn't that she didn't find him attractive; she did. He was very good-looking and friendly in a quiet sort of way. Whenever they worked together, they pretty much only talked about orders, work, and the occasional "what did you do on your day off?" that everyone did at work.

Pete came up and avoided making eye contact, as well. He spent time fawning over the bike, then fell silent. Esme wanted to speak to him, but had no clue where to start the conversation. She rang the bell again.

"It has a bell." Well, that sounded stupid.

"I see that," Pete replied, his ears turning red.

"Are you going home for the holidays?" Esme asked, repeating the simple conversations she overheard in the dining room when she was waitressing.

"Nah. I don't get on with my family. You?"

It seemed hard to believe Pete wouldn't get on with anyone. He was so soft spoken and kind, she imagined he could become a fly on the wall. She shook her head.

"No family."

Pete's brows rose, and he watched her for a moment. "I'm sorry. That must be hard."

Was it?

"I live at the halfway house a few streets over. We're having a nice dinner for those of us who don't have anywhere to go for the holidays."

As soon as she said halfway house, she regretted it. The only people in halfway houses were coming out of jail or the loony bin. At least, that's what people said. She heard it when she was leaving for work some days from people passing by. They didn't even try to hide their cruelty.

"Oh yeah? That's nice that they're having a dinner. I suppose I'll eat canned beans in my apartment," Pete said as a joke, but it sounded pained and lonely.

"No, you won't," a voice said behind them, making them both jump. Jo had scooted away when Pete first came over to see the bike, leaving them alone, but she'd made her reappearance. "My door's always open. You're welcome to have dinner at my place. Both of you are. I do a whole spread. Here, let me write down the details."

Esme wanted to come up with excuses why she couldn't attend, but found they died in her throat. She wanted to be wanted somewhere. The home was nice, but they were required to be there for the residents. Esme wanted to be a guest, not a burden.

Jo handed them each a piece of paper. "This is my address and what time to be there. My house is big with extra rooms, so if you decide you want to have a few drinks and stay the night, you are welcome to. I have a couple of loud and obnoxious little dogs, but they don't bite. All show. However, if they make you nervous, I can put them up."

Pete and Esme glanced at each other, then stared at the paper in their hands. Esme wondered how many people Jo invited over for dinner. Considering her personality, Esme assumed it was a lot. Was this a dinner or a party? What should she wear? Would it be awkward?

All of a sudden, the space they were standing in felt too small, and Esme needed a way out. She put her hands on the handlebars of the bike and began to push it outside. "I'm going to lock this to the bike rack out front. Thank you again, Jo. It means so much."

"Of course, hon. Please come to dinner. It will be small and easy. No fancy attire. We live free and easy," Jo said.

We? Was Jo married? She'd never mentioned a spouse, but then again, no one really talked about their lives outside of work. Maybe Jo was simply talking about her dogs; some people did that. Treated pets like family. Like children. That made more sense.

"I'll be there," Pete said. "Esme, do you want me to hold the door while you push your bike through?"

Esme nodded, glad for the distraction. She didn't want to make promises about going to dinner or hurt Jo's feelings. However, the idea of going to dinner with people she only knew at work was daunting. They pushed the bike outside and locked it to the bike rack.

Pete stopped to look up at the stars. "Do you ever think there are other beings out there? I mean, other than humans. Like we aren't alone?" he said, his voice wistful.

Esme was smart enough not to answer.

Chapter Seventeen

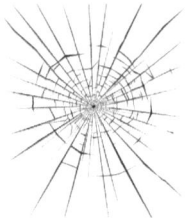

The night of the holiday dinner, Esme found herself beset by nerves. A new situation in a place she'd never been before. Sure, Jo and Pete would be there, but she hardly knew them either, and the budding feelings forming between her and Pete didn't help matters. She sat on her bed in her small room and clutched her bedspread, trying to work up the confidence to leave for the gathering. Pete had offered her a ride, but she decided taking her bike was the smarter choice. That way, she could leave if she needed to without inconveniencing him.

Elizabeth walked by her room and glanced in, then paused. "Are you alright, Esme? I thought you'd left for your party already."

Esme nodded. "Just working up the courage."

"Do you want to chat for a minute. I have time," Elizabeth offered.

"Sure. Not sure what to say, but it might help."

Elizabeth came into the room and sat on the desk chair. "What's making you worried?"

Esme considered the question. Was *everything* an answer? "I guess I know these people in my work environment, which is controlled. They know the Esme there, but not who I am really. Does that make sense?"

Elizabeth smiled. "Absolutely. We create personas for almost everywhere we are. Work, social situations, church, things like that. Work probably being one of the most restrictive because even the customer expects a version of us they are comfortable with. Sanitized even."

Sanitized. That was the perfect word for it. At work, Esme was polite, quiet, and fastidious. She never talked about her struggles or what happened in her private life. She'd slipped up the one time with Pete and mentioned she lived in the halfway house, but he'd been aware, or polite, enough to not press the issue.

However, at someone's home in a relaxed environment, people were bound to ask her personal questions. About herself, her family, her previous life. She wasn't ready to answer those questions. "What do I do if they ask me all sorts of things about myself I'm not ready to talk about?"

Elizabeth tipped her head, considering. "Well, decide what you *are* comfortable talking about and leave it at that. Practice a few questions and answers. If you aren't comfortable talking about something, be honest about it. Tell them there are things you'd rather not discuss."

Esme ran that idea over in her mind. Again, there was very little she wanted to discuss about herself because it opened the door to other things she definitely wasn't comfortable with. Maybe she could make up a story about her life they would believe.

As if Elizabeth read her mind, she leaned forward and whispered. "Just don't lie. That will create bigger issues than telling the truth or letting them know you aren't comfortable speaking about certain things. In the long run, if you decide to let these people into your world, lies will be hard to manage, and you could lose their trust."

Esme understood what Elizabeth was saying. However, the idea of having to share about herself or stand up and say she didn't want to scared her. Maybe she simply shouldn't go to the party. Elizabeth reached out and put her hand on Esme's, meeting her eyes.

"Eventually, you'll need to face the world and find your place in it, Esme. You can't run away from the hard stuff forever," she said, her eyes speaking the truth. "Go, have fun, and set your boundaries early on. If they don't like you doing that, then they aren't your people."

Elizabeth rose and went to the door, turning to smile at Esme. Esme smiled back, grateful for Elizabeth's patience and kind words. "Thank you, that really helped. I'm going to practice a few things with myself before I go. Ways to answer questions I'm worried about."

After Elizabeth left, Esme got up and went to stand in front of her mirror. She thought of common questions and came up with generic answers. No siblings, where she went to school, where she grew up before the hospital, interests, and general family questions. No lies, but some partial truths. Omissions really. She practiced diverting questions she wasn't comfortable with and ways to redirect the conversation.

She finished getting ready and went downstairs, waving at Sheena and Elizabeth as she left the house. Her bike was locked inside the front gate, and she unlocked it, slipping her purse into the daisy basket.

The ride to Jo's was a lot longer than she'd realized, and she arrived late, which made it even more awkward. Pete's car and a few others were parked in the driveway, so Esme pushed her bike past the vehicles and leaned it against the garage door out of sight.

Wandering back around front, Esme was surprised at the house size. It was a decent size, but she'd pictured a mansion. This was around the same size as the halfway house, though landscaped nicely and in much better condition. The flagstone front pathway was lit by solar lights and flowers, and curved unnecessarily through the front yard. Esme thought about walking off it in a straight line to the front porch, but considered that might be rude, so she meandered through the flowers on the stones until she arrived at the bottom step. It reminded her of the yellow brick road in The Wizard of Oz.

She ascended the stairs, her heart thumping in her chest. It wasn't too late to leave, she reminded herself. Even so, her feet kept climbing and her heart kept pounding away. She made it to the beautifully decorated door and pressed the dog-shaped doorbell. She could hear faint chatter and laughter from another part of the house and considered they hadn't heard the doorbell ring.

Panic set in, and she turned around, ready to bolt when the front door swung open wide. "Esme! You made it!"

Jo was standing in the doorway, a huge grin on her face. She wore a long, flowy silver gown and sandals, her gray-blond hair twisted up in a knot. Esme felt underdressed even though Jo had said it was casual.

"Your house is nice," Esme sputtered out, not sure what else to say.

"And you haven't even seen the inside. Come on in!"

Esme followed Jo into the house to a large living room, which was decorated with eclectic art pieces and lots and lots of books. Pete and another lady were there, looking at a coffee table art book. Pete glanced up and gave a short wave, his cheeks blushing. The other lady cocked her head, her eyes crinkling as she smiled.

"You must be Esme. I'm Linda. Jo has told me so much about you! Welcome to our home. We were just about to serve dinner, but were hoping you were about to arrive, and here you are!"

Their home? Was Linda Jo's sister, or roommate? Esme smiled and tried to quell her nerves. "Nice to meet you."

"Likewise. Dinner is ready, so let's move to the dining room. Our neighbors were going to join us, but their child is still napping. They may come over for dessert. They don't have much family, either. Apparently, her mother recently passed, so we thought it would be nice for them to come join us."

"They are a lovely little family, moved in recently. I hope they can pop over for a bit," Jo added.

Linda got up. "Let me show you to the dining room. Jo, do you need help bringing the food in?"

"No, honey. You show them where to sit and pour everyone a glass of wine. I'll bring the food right in," Jo replied.

Honey? Jo called Linda honey. Then again, she kind of called everyone honey. Pete and Esme followed Linda into the dining room and sat down across from each other, avoiding eye contact. A clatter came from the kitchen, followed by a very clear, "Damnit all to hell!"

Linda pointed to the wine. "Pete, pour you both a glass. Let me go help Jo."

Once she left, Pete got up and poured two glasses. Not only was Esme underage, she wasn't allowed to have alcohol with her meds. She smiled and pretended to take a sip. Pete sat back down and fiddled with his glass, also not drinking.

Esme gazed at where Linda had disappeared, then back at Pete. "Jo and Linda are...?"

"They are a couple," Pete jumped in.

"Oh." Esme felt weird about that, but she wasn't sure why. It didn't bother her, but still she felt strange about it.

"Are you okay with that?" Pete asked, clearly reading her response as not being okay.

"I think so. I just hadn't considered it," Esme replied, telling the truth. "They seem happy together."

Pete nodded. "I was surprised when I got here, too. Jo never said anything about her home life. Well, except the dogs. Linda seems really nice."

A few moments later, Linda and Jo came back in carrying platters of food. Jo winked. "I promise I didn't dump our food on the ground. Well, I knocked over a platter of rolls, but luckily I had fresh ones."

Throughout dinner, the conversation flowed, but they never asked more questions than Esme was comfortable answering. Practicing her answers helped her feel confident in her responses, and Linda and Jo were both big talkers, so they moved on quickly in the conversation. Esme kept her answers simple and left out any details that might open the door to more questions. Pete seemed to be doing the same.

Jo and Linda, however, were open books. They talked about how they met in college and traveled the world. How they decided to settle in that town because Jo had grown up there. She'd always wanted to own a pizza parlor because, as a kid, there had never been one in the town. Linda was a professor at the nearby college and, from what it sounded like, kept the bills paid while the pizza place grew roots in the community.

After dinner, they moved to the living room to have coffee and dessert. Esme noticed Pete hadn't drunk his wine, either. They settled on the large couches, and Jo turned on the radio for sound. Classical music eased out, making the room seem even more cozy.

Jo brought in dessert and set it on the coffee table. "Baklava. It's divine with coffee. You can eat it with your fingers, or I brought some dessert forks in if you'd prefer."

Esme eyed the pastry, then cleared her throat. "Where is your restroom?"

"Just down the hall, first door on the left."

Esme excused herself and went to the bathroom. While she was inside the small room, she heard the doorbell and assumed it was the neighbors coming for dessert. She wasn't keen on meeting more new people, but didn't want to be impolite. She opened the door and went down the hall, her ears tuned into the conversation going on.

She heard a man's voice introducing himself to Pete, then a woman's voice chiming in. She knew that voice. Esme's blood ran cold, and she froze in the hallway, not sure what to do. She pressed against the wall and craned her neck to see the people in the living room. Seeing what she was afraid to, Esme broke out into a sweat.

Becky and Mario were standing in Jo's living room.

Chapter Eighteen

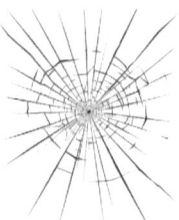

E sme peered out through the opening and knew she couldn't face them. So it *must* have been Mario she saw walking past the restaurant that day. Becky and Mario were the neighbors Jo and Linda were speaking about. They had moved to the town. Now that Esme thought about it, Mario could have lived there to work at the hospital. She wasn't sure why she assumed he'd moved in with Becky and Aunt Darla.

Aunt Darla.

Jo said the female neighbor's mother had recently died. If the female neighbor was Becky, then Aunt Darla had passed away. She wasn't that old, Esme thought. No older than Jo or Linda. A wave of sadness passed over Esme, and she leaned against the wall, trying to pull herself together. Now what?

As if to answer her question, Esme heard Jo say to Mario and Becky, "Esme should be right out. She just ran to the bathroom."

Esme panicked and held her breath, as if breathing would give her location away. Becky gasped and whispered, "Did you say Esme?"

"I did. Do you know her?" Jo asked.

"I... I'm not sure. What does she look like?" Becky replied, her voice tight.

"Long, dark, wavy hair. Freckles. Around twenty years old. I mean, she should be right out," Jo said.

Esme ran down the hall, looking for an escape route out of the house other than the front door. She couldn't face Becky. She turned and found herself in a small bedroom. She ran to the windows and tried pushing them up. The first one didn't budge, but the second one slid up easily. Esme kicked the screen out and scrambled through the opening, pitching face-first onto the ground. Stunned, she stumbled to her feet, hearing Jo calling her name.

Esme darted around to the garage and grabbed her bike, jumping on it and pedaling out of the driveway. No one saw her as they were still searching inside the house for her. Esme felt tears streaming down her cheeks and pedaled faster, as if to outrun her past.

It was dark out, and she struggled to see the road in front of her, the bike wheels hitting the edge of the road and throwing her off. Esme tumbled into a ditch and lay there for a moment, wishing she were dead. Headlights coming down the road illuminated her, and she pressed down into the ditch to try to not be seen. However, the driver must have spotted her bike and pulled over.

"Esme?" a man's voice called out. Not Mario, Pete.

Esme sat up and pushed her hair out of her face, knowing there was no way to hide from him. Pete saw her in the ditch and frowned. "Esme! Are you hurt? Did you crash your bike?"

She shook her head and stood up. "Just scratches and bruises. How did you find me?"

"Well, you said you lived near the pizza place, so I figured if I drove in that direction, I might find you. What happened back there?" Pete asked and set her bike upright, leaning it on the kickstand.

Esme needed to tell someone. She was tired of hiding all the time and running. "That lady who came to the house? She is my cousin."

Pete's face dropped in disbelief, and he pushed her bike over to his car. "Here, let me give you a ride home. She's your family?"

"She is. We don't talk anymore, though."

Pete paused and nodded as he scanned her face. "I believe you. You want a ride?"

Esme sighed and bobbed her head. "Thank you. That would be nice."

Pete loaded her bike, then opened the passenger door for Esme. She climbed in and noticed his car was very clean. No food wrappers, no drink cans, no dust or clutter. He went around to the driver's side and got in. He smiled at her. "Just tell me where to go."

Esme gave him directions, then fell silent. He said he believed her, but he was still acting strange. She stared at his profile in the dashboard lights. "Why did you leave their house to come find me?"

Pete glanced at her. "Well, you left without telling anyone, so I assumed something happened to make you leave. We saw your bike was gone, so I left immediately. The neighbors were acting freaked out, and Jo and Linda were trying to talk to them to understand why."

Esme knew why. "They heard my name and knew it was me. That's why I had to leave. I couldn't face them."

"What happened between you?" Pete asked, keeping his eyes on the road.

"It's not that simple, Pete. I have problems, things you don't know about. That's why I live in the halfway house."

"You seem fine to me," he countered.

"Before the halfway house, I was committed to the mental hospital," Esme added, pushing the conversation. It felt good to say it out loud.

Pete's eyes widened, but he quickly set his face back to a neutral state. "That happens sometimes. I get depressed and anxious."

"It's not like that. I have episodes sometimes. See or do things I can't explain."

Pete pulled the car over and cut off the lights, turning to face Esme. "Do you want to talk about it?"

For the first time, Esme did. She told him everything about her mother dying in childbirth, her father committing suicide when she was small, then Uncle Ray dying unexpectedly. She talked about being picked on in school by Sara and how things unfolded the day by the buses, but left out the part of Sara's death. How all of it made her feel like a stranger in the world and even in her own life. She told him about the incident with Becky at the hospital, as well, after finding out about the pregnancy. Pete listened and never acted more than a little surprised. Esme did leave out her imaginary, or not so imaginary, companions and what she suspected they did. That seemed like too much to share. She also didn't mention Allison at all.

Once she stopped talking, Pete rubbed his chin and stared out the windshield. Esme was ready for him to take her home and never want to speak to her again. Instead, he nodded and took her hand.

"Sounds to me like you were dealt a bad hand from birth, and that's a lot to deal with for anyone. First your mother, then your father, then your uncle dying. That would break most people. From what you told me, Sara was bullying you, and you reacted. Maybe overreacted, but who's to say what we do in that kind of situation? My father beat us kids severely growing up. It was relentless. I ran away at fourteen and never went back. As for Becky, I think you felt betrayed and lashed out at her. However, they wouldn't have let you leave if you hadn't made progress, gotten better, right?"

Esme felt he was trying to make excuses for her behaviour, which she knew wasn't right, but it also felt good to have someone believe in her. "Right."

He squeezed her hand. "So, let's get you home, and don't worry too much about it. I'm sure Becky already filled Jo in on your relationship, so Jo will understand why you left. You can talk to her when you get back to work."

Esme balked. "I can't go back to the pizza place!"

"Why not?" Pete asked gently.

"Because now Jo knows everything about me. About how screwed up I am," Esme answered.

"You aren't screwed up. You went through some shit, that's all. I'll talk to her first, alright?"

Esme watched him and felt the tension release. "Alright. Pete, why are you so nice to me?"

Pete's brows knitted. "Don't you know how I feel about you, Esme?"

She knew she caught him watching her sometimes and that he was always nice to her, but Esme didn't understand the level of his feelings. "Not really."

Pete chuckled and blushed. "I like you, Esme. I want to take you on dates and get to know you better. I've been working up the courage to ask you out."

Now Esme blushed. "Oh. Okay."

"Okay, you'll go out with me?" Pete asked, his voice unsure.

"Yes. If you still want to after what I told you."

Pete leaned over and kissed her cheek. "Like I said, you just went through some stuff. I can't fault you for that. So did I. I did some things I wasn't proud of, as well."

"Like what?"

Pete shook his head. "Stupid stuff. Breaking into people's homes, stealing stuff. Drinking too much and doing drugs. Too many drugs. I don't do that anymore, though. I've been sober for thirteen months."

"That's why you didn't drink tonight?"

"You noticed?" Pete asked, surprised.

Esme nodded. "I don't drink, either, but because it interferes with my meds. You poured both of us a glass of wine, but neither of us drank ours. Why did you pour one for yourself if you don't drink?"

"It's easier that way. If I pour something and have it in front of me, people don't ask why I don't drink, and I don't have to explain my life story."

Esme could understand that. Pete was still holding her hand, and she liked it, but also was afraid he'd forgotten and didn't want to be. She wiggled her fingers, and he squeezed her hand again. He let go and started the car.

"Do you want to go home?"

Esme didn't, but she was tired and needed to regroup after the activity of the evening. "Yes, please. Thank you. Can we do this again soon, maybe when I didn't freak out and run out of our boss's house?"

Pete laughed, and she enjoyed the sound of it. "Of course. How about a real date? I'll take you to dinner."

"That sounds nice. As long as it isn't pizza," Esme replied with a chuckle.

"Got it. No pizza, no boss's house. Just you and me at a non-Italian restaurant. Deal?"

"Deal." Esme smiled to herself. She liked Pete and didn't feel like she had to pretend to be someone else when she was around him.

Sort of.

There were still secrets she kept. She didn't want to scare him off before they really had a chance to get to know one another. They pulled up in front of the halfway house, and Pete parked the car. He faced Esme.

"Thank you for letting me give you a ride home. Let me get your bike out and walk you to the door."

Before Esme could protest, Pete was out the driver's door and had the bike sitting on the curb. He opened Esme's door and extended his hand. She smiled and took it. They locked her bike to the front fence and walked up the path to the house. Pete stopped at the stoop and leaned in to kiss Esme's cheek. She felt blood rush to her face and dropped her eyes, feeling vulnerable. Pete tipped her chin up with his fingers and grinned.

"Have a good night, Esme."

She nodded and rushed inside, afraid she'd say something stupid and ruin the moment. She shut the front door and glanced up the stairs. A shadow moved on the stairwell, then disappeared. Esme caught her breath. Was someone watching her?

When she got to her room, she froze at the door. Her room had been destroyed. Her clothes and bedding were thrown everywhere, and her journal was torn up, strewn all over the room. Esme stared in shock, sensing the hair rise on the back of her neck. Movement caught her eye, and she glanced over toward it.

The shadow snickered and disappeared into the closet.

Chapter Nineteen

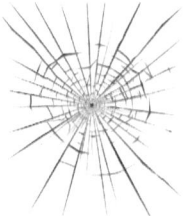

Despite the destroyed room and the closet shadow she witnessed that night, Esme continued to progress at the halfway house, working the job and enrolling in community college. Jo never brought up Becky or that night; she also didn't treat Esme any differently after the incident. Esme could only imagine what Becky and Mario told Jo about her. She was surprised Jo didn't fire her on the spot when she showed up two days later for her shift.

When she mentioned wanting to go to school, Jo offered to help cover some of the tuition. Grants covered the rest. Within a few months, Esme was excelling in her classes, despite working full-time. She decided she eventually wanted to be a veterinarian and enrolled in vet tech classes to get started toward that goal.

She knew it was coming time to leave the halfway house and began searching for cheap apartments. She and Pete had been seeing each other since the night at Jo's, so he suggested they move in together. They hadn't done more than make out in his car, and she felt even that was moving too fast for her. Pete was her first boyfriend, and it was becoming serious at lightning speed.

"I think I need to learn to be on my own first," she answered, trying to let him down easy.

Pete looked disappointed, however, he'd been on his own since he was fourteen and couldn't begrudge her that chance at independence. "You know I'm just going to be over there all the time, though, right?"

Esme laughed. "I know, Pete. Still. I have never lived on my own and need to learn who I am without someone else around."

"That's very mature of you, Esme. I won't lie, I'm a little bummed, but I know I'll wear you down over time," he teased with a wink.

She knew he would, too. Being with Pete made her forget about her past, and except for the shadow who now lived in her closet and tore up her things sometimes, she felt almost normal.

The shadow wasn't like her other companions. It never interacted with her. While she was at school or work, it would rearrange her room, hide her things, and destroy her personal creations. However, as soon as she came home, it disappeared into the closet, not to emerge again until she left. Sometimes she heard it crying in there. Soft sobs peppered with sniffs and whispers she couldn't make out.

The halfway house only allowed residents to stay for up to a year in order to help them find a way on their own, so as the one-year anniversary of her arrival drew near, Esme hurried to find a place to live. She settled on a small, one-bedroom apartment above a dry cleaner in town. It was around halfway between the college and the pizza place. A new *halfway* house, she told Pete, and he laughed.

"Leave it to you to find humor in everyday life things," he responded, brushing her hair off her shoulder and kissing her exposed skin there.

When Pete touched her, Esme felt alive. They wanted to take it to the next level, but not until she'd moved into her own place. She sighed and leaned back against the car seat. They spent most of their time in there, as Pete had a nosy roommate who hung around any time Esme was over. Pete said he thought his roommate had a thing for her. Esme did too, as the older man would leer at her when she was there.

"I move in next Wednesday," she said, touching his cheek as he sat back.

"Do you need help?"

"With what?"

"Moving your stuff."

"Oh, I don't really have stuff. The furniture in my room belongs to the halfway house. I have my books, clothes, and some small things. That's about it," Esme replied.

"Where are you going to sleep, then?" Pete asked, surprised.

Esme hadn't really considered that part of moving. She had nothing to put in the apartment to start with. All of her money was used for the deposit and the first month's rent, as well. "I don't know."

"If we moved in together..."

"I know, Pete. I'm just not ready. Let me ask Jo and check out some thrift stores. I want to do this right. You're my first boyfriend, I don't want to mess this up between us," Esme replied, finding courage in her words.

"We'll find you some furniture in the meantime. At least a bed, right?" Pete replied with a smile. "I can't have my girl sleeping on the floor."

On her next shift, Esme asked Jo if she knew of anywhere she could find cheap or free furniture and dishes. Jo grinned and pulled out a box of plates and kitchenware.

"Extras from when we set up the restaurant. We don't need them, so now you at least have something to cook with and eat off of. I'll talk to Linda to see if we have any furniture we can spare. You should have a housewarming party," Jo suggested.

"What's that?"

"Oh, a housewarming party?. It's where you invite people over for a gathering to celebrate your new space, and they bring things for your home. I'll set it up!"

A housewarming party. For some reason, that sounded greedy to Esme, but Jo seemed excited about it. She did need stuff, and Jo acted like everyone did this all the time, so she smiled and nodded. "Thanks, Jo."

"What do you have so far?" Jo asked, grabbing a piece of paper and a pen. "We'll make a list."

Esme grinned and pointed at the box. "Looks like some plates and kitchen things."

Jo leaned her head back and laughed. "Alright then, so everything."

Later that night in her room, Esme heard the shadow crying again and crept over to the closet to listen. She could hear it murmuring to itself, but couldn't make out the words it was saying.

Feeling sorry for it, Esme leaned in close to the door. "Are you okay in there?"

The shadow fell quiet. Esme could still hear it breathing. Do shadows breathe? She thought maybe if she talked to it, it would stop ruining her things.

"My name is Esme. This is my room. That is my closet. Where did you come from?'

No answer.

Esme wrinkled her brow. She reached for the door and turned the knob. The breathing stopped. Easing the door open, Esme peered in, not seeing the shadow. "Hello? Are you in there?"

No answer.

Esme opened the door wider. "I'm moving soon. Next week. You can have my room and this closet all to yourself then. Is that why you keep rearranging my stuff? You want the room to be yours?"

No answer.

The closet appeared empty, and Esme rotated to look around the room. No shadow. The light from her lamp cast a glow on Esme, and she could see she had her own shadow. She raised her hand and waved it, watching her shadow dance along the wall. So the closet shadow wasn't hers. She turned back, hand still in the air, and saw movement in the closet. The shadow was standing toward the back with its hand in the air.

Like Esme.

It wasn't her shadow, but she suddenly got the feeling it wanted to be. She supposed it was destroying her things because it was jealous of her shadow. No, more than that. Jealous of Esme and her freedom. She chewed her lip.

"Where did you come from?"

No answer.

"Did you hear me? I'm leaving next week."

The shadow grew larger, taking up the back wall of the closet. Esme glanced at her shadow along the wall outside the closet, stretched out from the glow. Part of her. Benign. Not like the shadow in the closet, which seemed to have a mind of its own.

"I don't understand why you came here? Where are you from?" she asked, trying to coax the shadow to interact with her.

No answer.

"Okay, well, I need to get some sleep. I'll be out of your hair soon," she told the shadow. It remained with its hand raised as she closed the door.

Esme climbed into bed, hearing the shadow resume its low, soft sobbing. She felt for it but didn't know what else to do. She dozed off dreaming of her new apartment. Her new life. A chance at a fresh start.

Late in the night, the sound of shifting around her woke her up. She opened her eyes and saw the shadow was moving her desk to a different wall. She sat up, confused. It never did that when she was in the room. It dragged the furniture noisily across the floorboards, and Esme wondered how it didn't wake everyone else up.

"Hello? Stop that," she said.

The shadow ignored her and kept dragging. Esme climbed out of bed and walked toward the dark figure. It turned as she neared, tense and still.

Esme reached out to touch the shadow, but her hand fell into its inky blackness. No, it wasn't a shadow, after all. The blackness crept slowly up her arm to her shoulder and began to pull on her. She tried to scream, but it absorbed her into itself until she was being sucked into a strange tunnel made from cosmic space.

Everything and everyone she knew passed by her as she tumbled without gravity through the endless abyss. Gone was her room and her place in the world. She now belonged to the darkness. No, the being in her closet was not a shadow. It was something much more formidable. Something Esme was powerless to fight against.

A black hole.

Chapter Twenty

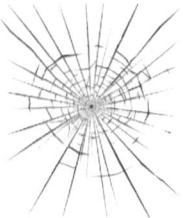

E sme tumbled uncontrolled through the darkness, then found herself suspended between worlds. She reached out and could feel the air around her between her fingers. It had an oily, almost gelatinous texture, and she wondered how she could be breathing the thick substance. Her eyes could find no light to adjust to. She shifted around in the viscosity and attempted to get her bearings.

"Hello?" she called out.

The air around her rippled like a pebble dropped in a pond. She was now inside the shadow that inhabited her closet. Using her arms in a swimming motion, Esme found if she could get them to sync in movement, she could propel herself forward or back. After a few minutes of this, she realized it didn't make much of a difference to her current state of being. She remained in the stagnant nothingness. There was no forward or back, only suspension.

Why?

Why had the shadow brought her there? Where exactly was she? Esme closed her eyes, not that it mattered, and listened. She thought she heard muffled voices in the distance and honed in on what they were saying. Their words weren't clear, but the tone was. The voices were strained and angry. Two voices, a man and a woman. No matter how hard she tried, Esme couldn't make out what they were saying, only the back and forth of the different pitches of their voices.

Anxiety surged through Esme, and it felt like the very air, the substance, around her changed in response to the voices. Became thicker, harder to move around in. Esme fought against the density, tiring herself out. Finally, she rested and allowed the air to hold her in place.

The voices faded, and Esme drifted off to sleep, being awoken a short time later by the space around her vibrating. A salty wetness hit her lips, and she recoiled, not comprehending where it came from. She brushed her lips to wipe it away, but found her hand clumsy and ineffective.

The vibrating stopped, and Esme felt a strange warm glow come over her. For a moment, she felt she wasn't alone in the darkness. A soft hum, different from the vibration echoed through her containment, and she listened, finding comfort in the sound.

A connection.

In this state, Esme began to have visions. Of being weightless and surrounded by lights. She remembered hearing people speak about being abducted by aliens. Was that what happened?

Something inside her said it wasn't, however, she understood she needed to go deeper to understand. She allowed the visions to draw her in and found herself in a large, open room with other beings. Not exactly people, because like her, they were not in human bodies. Yet she could recognize their individualness, their existence as a being.

Esme found she was no longer suspended in the darkness and could move around the space with the others. Each of them seemed to be working and focusing on a task, but Esme could not define what exactly they were doing. It seemed to make sense, yet she couldn't explain why.

It simply did.

Staring at her hands, she recognized she also wasn't in the form she recognized. She was still her, in a different form. Like the beings around her, she was and she wasn't.

"Hello?" she called out again. Or thought she did, but the words seemed to evaporate into nothing as soon as they left her... her mouth?

No response. The others around her stayed absorbed in their tasks, seemingly unaware of her presence near them. It was peaceful and felt natural to be there. Like worry didn't exist. Esme watched as one by one, they were drawn from their spots and disappeared into the nothingness.

Something tugged at her, and she was back in the dark space. Alone and scared. Was she going to be there forever? The walls around her began to vibrate again, this time more violently. It felt like the thick air around her was suffocating as Esme fought against the constricting enclosure. It continued to draw inward, squeezing her and forcing her into a smaller space. She couldn't breathe and thrust her arms out, beating on the pressure around her. She was dying, she was sure of it.

Just as Esme gave up fighting and accepted her fate, closing her eyes to the inevitable, she jerked awake. She was in her bed in the halfway house, covered in sweat. She ran her hands down her arms and shivered, the room feeling unusually cold. As she drew her hands away, she noticed the sweat had a different texture. Almost a little tacky. Not sweat, something else. Like the atmosphere in the space she'd been trapped in by the shadow.

Esme climbed out of bed and clicked on a light. Glancing at her body, nothing seemed out of the ordinary except for the coating of fluid on her. It was clear and didn't have a smell, but it felt like the air in the nothingness. It was in her hair, as well.

Esme peeked down the hall to make sure no one was out there, then slipped into the bathroom to take a shower. She had no idea what time it was or how long she'd been.. been what? Dreaming? Gone?

Turning the shower on for it to heat up, Esme peered into the mirror at herself. Her pupils seemed odd, dilated. She ran her fingers down her cheeks and attempted to connect with the girl in the mirror. The girl stared blankly back at her with disinterest. Esme wasn't sure it was even herself looking back at her.

Slipping out of her clothes, Esme stepped into the shower and sighed as the hot water rinsed her clean. She scrubbed her skin until it was bright red and washed her hair three times to make sure whatever she'd been covered in was completely gone. Once she was sure she was clean, Esme cut off the shower and stood in the stall, letting the water run off her down the drain.

A soft knock came at the door as Esme got out of the shower, wrapping a towel around her. The knock came again, and Esme called out, "I'll be done in a minute."

"Esme? It's Lisa. Are you alright in there?"

"Yes, just taking a shower. I'm almost done," Esme replied, trying to hurry in case she took someone else's shower slot. She scooped up her clothes, holding them away from her as they were still damp with whatever fluid she'd been covered in. Unlocking the door, she opened it to see Lisa standing there with a concerned look on her face.

"Are you alright?" Lisa asked again.

Esme was confused. Did she look weird or something? "Yeah, I was grabbing a quick shower before school."

Lisa frowned. "It's two-thirty in the morning, Esme."

That would explain why Lisa was acting so strange. Esme shook her head and lied. "Oh, I must have read my clock wrong. I thought it was five o'clock when I got up. I guess I'll go lie back down for a bit."

Lisa looked like she didn't believe Esme, but moved to let her pass by. "Okay. Let me know if you need anything. I am reading in the living room."

Esme nodded and hurried down the hall, embarrassed. She knew Lisa saw through the lie. She slipped into her room, shutting the door behind her. Dropping her clothes in the hamper, she felt her sheets and realized they too were covered in the strange substance. She stripped the sheets, throwing them in the hamper. She grabbed a fresh set out of the closet, pulling the string for the light in the small space.

The shadow was gone. For good, she didn't know. For now, it appeared like an ordinary closet. She took a set of sheets down off the shelf and went to turn off the light when she realized she felt better with it on. Shadow or not, she sensed she was being watched.

After slipping on pajamas and changing her sheets, Esme crawled into bed, exhausted. She had classes in a few hours and needed to get some sleep. She closed her eyes and allowed the draw of rest to pull her in. Surprised she was able to drift off so easily, Esme let go.

When she woke up, the sun was high in the sky, and she realized she'd missed her first class. She hurried to get dressed and grabbed her books, hoping she wouldn't run into anyone on the way out. After running into Lisa last night, she didn't want to be asked twenty questions about what was going on with her. She bolted down the stairs into the bright sun, unlocking her bike from the fence as she slipped her books into the basket. She pushed the bike out to the street and peered back at the house. She swore she saw someone in one of the upper windows, but couldn't be sure it wasn't only a trick of the light.

The sun was blinding as she pedalled as hard as she could toward the college, forgetting about anything except making it to school on time. With the sun in her eyes, she could barely make out what was around her and noticed the people walking on the sidewalk looked sort of like the beings from her dream, or experience... whatever it was. Bright and semi-shapeless, moving mindlessly throughout their daily tasks. This drew her back into what happened in the abyss, and she missed a stop sign in front of her.

She didn't even see when the car hit her.

Chapter Twenty-One

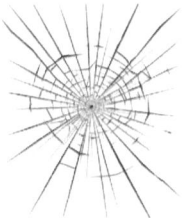

"**C**an you hear me?" a voice from afar said.

Esme tried to open her eyes and move but her body screamed in pain with any motion. Her head felt split open, and her eyes wouldn't crack open more than a slit. Even so, she could make out movement around her. She attempted to speak, but only gurgling came out.

"Don't try to move, miss. The ambulance is on its way," the voice told her.

Esme couldn't breathe and began to panic. Something was blocking her airway. She sensed a buildup of pressure in her lungs and desperately tried to suck in air. To no avail.

"She's not breathing!" a different voice yelled. "What do we do?"

"The ambulance should be here any minute," the first voice replied.

"She might not have that long. She's suffocating," the second voice said, their voice strained. "We have to do something to help her now!"

Esme *was* suffocating. Her lungs and brain screamed for air. She heard shuffling around her and her neck being tipped slightly back.

"What are you doing? Just wait for the ambulance," the first voice stated.

"No. She may not make it long enough for them to arrive. We need to help her before she dies. I've seen this done on TV."

"On TV? Are you serious? You could kill her!"

"She's going to die if I don't. Get out of my way," the second voice demanded.

All of a sudden, a sharp pain hit Esme's neck. A burning, jabbing pain. The voice grunted, and she could feel someone's hands bracing her head as the pressure on her throat increased exponentially. She wanted to scream out, but couldn't. The pain retracted for a second, and a new sensation came. Pain, pressure, but not as much as before. All of a sudden, a thin stream of air made its way into her lungs. Not a deep breath, but enough to keep her from feeling like she was dying. She wanted more, but the stream wouldn't increase.

"Is she breathing?" the first asked.

"I think so. Look, her face is going back to a more normal color."

"Damn, you really did it," the first voice muttered in surprise. "I couldn't have done that."

A few minutes later, sirens grew in the distance. Esme felt her body was starving for more air, but she knew whatever they did to her neck kept her from completely suffocating. The sirens became louder, and Esme could hear them come to a stop close by. Voices were yelling all around her, but she couldn't make out what they were saying.

Hands began to check her over, careful not to move her body too much. Esme felt something poking her fingers and other parts of her body. She flinched with each one. A gruff woman's voice near her called out. "Who did the street tracheotomy?"

"Uh, me," the second voice replied sheepishly. "She was suffocating, and I was afraid she'd die before you got here. I didn't have a choice."

"I see. What did you use to cut the hole?"

"A pocket knife. Then I put the tube of a pen in there."

"That much I can see," the gruff voice replied. "Well, it did the trick. Sloppy and dangerous, but she's breathing. Mike, let's get her moved onto the gurney. Doesn't appear to be any spinal damage."

Hands slid her over onto a retracted gurney. Then it was raised up and she felt the wheels move across the bumpy asphalt.

A different man's voice spoke. "Where's the driver of the car? I need to speak to him."

"Over there, officer," the first voice replied. "He's pretty shaken up. Said she came flying through a stop sign, and he didn't have time to hit the brakes. He's really upset and blaming himself."

"Did you see the accident?" the officer asked.

"No, sir. Just going off what he said. I got here a few seconds later."

"Alright, go ahead and take a step back to let them get her loaded into the ambulance. How about you? Did you see anything?"

The second voice spoke up. "I did, but I was a little ways off. I was coming down the street the other way when I saw the car hit her, and she went flying into the air."

"Did either of you check her for any kind of identification?"

Mumbling voices said they hadn't, but the officer called out. "Hey, Mike, check her for identification. She looks young; her parents might be worried."

Esme was young, but her parents weren't worried. They didn't even exist anymore. Esme felt a needle slip into her arm, and within a minute, she felt some pain relief.

The gruff woman's voice spoke over the top of her. "You're going to be alright, hon. Hang in there. We're getting you to the hospital as quickly as we can. We're leaving this make-shift tracheotomy in until we get there. You're going to need surgery. Squeeze my hand if you understand what I am telling you."

Esme felt the weight of the woman's hand in her own. She tried to squeeze it, not sure if she was doing anything. The woman clasped her hand tightly, and Esme focused on that. The ambulance started up, and Esme felt the shifting of the gurney as it took off down the road, sirens blaring.

Everything else happened in fragments. The woman said her name was Kelly. The ambulance came to a stop. The gurney was rolled out from the back. They were in the hospital. Voices talking. Beeping. Flashing lights. More hands touching her.

The next thing Esme remembered was waking up in the surgical recovery room, everything on fire in her body. Her throat burned and was bandaged. Esme tried to speak, but unspeakable pain silenced her. Her eyes were still swollen mostly shut, only allowing the degrees of light through, so she was left with using her ears to understand what was going on.

Someone, a young man, came over and took her pulse. "Esme? Is that your name? We found your school ID in your bag. No address or emergency contacts, though. However, a search in the system alerted us that Dr. Hubach was your doctor. We have contacted him to try and find your family."

Esme wanted to scream to stop them, but not even a whisper came out of her throat. Dr. Hubach would likely contact Becky since she was her only family, and Esme didn't want that. She'd rather be alone.

The young man cleared his throat. "Dr. Daniels, her blood pressure is going up. Can you come take a look?"

A calloused hand pressed on her wrist, and she felt a cold piece of metal against her chest. An old man's voice spoke. "Keep an eye on it for now. She's waking up, which can spike her blood pressure for a bit. However, we can give her medication to bring it down if it doesn't come on its own. Any word from family?"

"No, sir. We are waiting on a call back from her doctor."

"Her doctor? What kind of doctor?"

The young man's voice lowered like he was telling a dirty secret. "Psychiatrist."

"Ah, I see. Alright, well, let me know when you do. In the meantime, see if she can be moved into a more private space. She might be getting stressed from all the activity in here and not understand what is going on."

Once again, Esme felt herself being moved. This time, she was in a quieter room, but she could tell she wasn't alone. The sound of machines and someone coughing let her know the room was shared.

Esme went in and out of consciousness for some time. What amount, she didn't know because she couldn't see or speak. It felt like days, however, she had no way of knowing. Often, hands would come in and check on her, move her, change her, touch her. She had the sensation of being a baby, unable to fend for herself.

After many cycles of going in and out, Esme found she could open her eyes enough to at least tell if it was dark or light out and make out shapes. She still couldn't speak and didn't know how long it would be until she could.

At one of the light times, she heard the room door open and assumed it was someone coming to visit her roommate, however, the person came and sat down next to her bed. A soft voice coughed gently, then spoke.

"Esme, it's Becky. I know you don't want me here, and to be honest, I wasn't sure I was coming. But we are family, and I needed to at least let you know you weren't alone. They said you had a tracheostomy that damaged your vocal cords, so I don't expect you to speak. Your right leg is shattered, as well. Lots of other things, but I'm sure you know that. I want you to know we'll make sure your hospital bills are taken care of. Mario's mother passed and left him a bit of money. He cares about you, Esme. He always did. I'm so sorry we messed up and didn't talk to you about our relationship. We love each other very much and want you to be part of our family."

It sounded like Becky was speaking more to herself than Esme, but Esme listened, wanting to put the past behind her and find a way to bridge the gap between them. She tried to open her eyes more and focus on Becky, but she couldn't make out more than a shadow of her cousin.

Becky sat for a while, then sighed. "I wish I knew if you wanted me here. I don't want to invade your privacy, but I love you, Esme. I hope you know that. I spoke to Jo. She said you're seeing that boy, Pete, who was over at the house that night, and she would let him know what happened to you, as well. Please get better, Esme. I'd like to have another chance to be your family."

Becky rose and touched Esme's arm before she left. Esme listened to her retreating footsteps and let go of the tension she'd been holding in while Becky was there. She wanted family, too, but she still couldn't trust Becky. She couldn't trust herself. She let her eyes close and sank back into the darkness.

"That your sister?" her roommate asked. The person's voice was female and sounded about Esme's age.

Esme couldn't answer but shook her head.

"No? You kind of look alike. Are you related, though?"

Esme nodded.

"I thought so. You didn't seem happy that she was here. Did she do something to you?"

Esme found the questions intrusive but figured if she didn't answer, her roommate would keep asking. She shrugged in response.

"Yeah? Seemed like it. I'm Felicia. Stuck here until my kidneys heal. Well, this time around anyway. Genetic renal disease. A real bitch to be trapped in the hospital at nineteen years old, but I've been dealing with it my whole life. You're Esme? I heard the nurse say your name."

Esme nodded and turned her head away to try and send the message she didn't want to talk anymore. Talk? No, she couldn't even squeak out a grunt.

"Sorry, I know, a lot of questions. I get lonely in here a lot. I spend way too much time in the hospital. I was glad when they brought you into the room. I'll leave you alone. Nice to have someone here around my age, though. Hopefully, you can talk soon."

Esme sincerely doubted it.

Chapter Twenty-Two

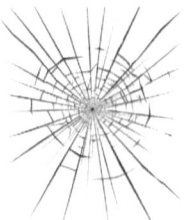

By the time Esme could open her eyes, she was sick of being stuck in bed. The first morning she realized she was seeing the hospital room around her, she peered around, putting together the pieces of what she'd heard with what she was seeing. Her roommate was asleep diagonally across from her. Esme stared at the small woman. Girl? She was curled up with her back to Esme, but Esme could make out certain characteristics. Blonde hair but with dark olive skin. She said she was nineteen years old. Esme remembered that much.

Felicia. She was chatty, and Esme still couldn't speak. The doctors told her that her throat needed time to heal. They also said there was a chance she might not regain her voice, and if she did, it might sound different. The tracheotomy saved her life but took her voice. Maybe.

Felicia rolled over and yawned, opening her bright green eyes that stood out against her deep tan skin. When she saw Esme looking at her, she sat up and grinned. "Hey! Your eyes are open!"

Esme nodded and pointed at her throat. Felicia tipped her head. "Cat got your tongue? Just kidding. We can pass notes back and forth now that you can see."

Esme wasn't sure how that would work since she couldn't get out of bed on her own yet. Felicia seemed to have moved on to something else. She clicked on the television.

"You like TV? I'm addicted to it. If I'm awake, it has to be on. You know?"

Esme knew. Not personally, but because Felicia always had it going. The television in the room ran from sunup to sundown, and from what it sounded like, Felicia didn't care what was on. In fact, she seemed to like watching shopping channels, which Esme detested. The high-pitched fake voices going on and on about some piece of junk or another. Even so, she forced a smile and bobbed her head. Felicia adjusted the TV so it faced Esme a little more. Esme hoped she'd be able to mentally block it out.

Later that day, when Felicia was out for physical therapy, Pete stopped by the room. He hadn't come by yet, and Esme wasn't thrilled he was there now. She looked like... well, like she'd been hit by a car. Pete came in holding a bunch of grocery store daisies and gazed around for something to put them in. Finally, giving up, he laid them on the table beside Esme's bed and gazed at her. His face appeared apologetic.

"Hey, Esme. How are you feeling?" His words sounded practiced and a little nervous.

Esme pointed at her throat and wrote on a pad of paper. "Can't talk. Doctors say I may never be able to."

Pete read the note and frowned. "Ever?"

Esme shrugged. She wrote another note. "Maybe. I'm supposed to let it heal. How's everything at work?"

"Busy. I'm covering your shifts when I can. Jo is making sure you have a job to come back to."

This surprised Esme, as she figured business was business and Jo would have to replace her. She smiled and scribbled down more words. "Tell her thank you. She doesn't have to do that. I had to give up my apartment."

"Why?"

"They wouldn't hold it past the first of the month. Also, it's on the third floor, and it might be a while before I can climb stairs again."

"What are you going to do when you leave the hospital, then?" Pete asked.

"I don't know."

"You can always move in with me. I'm in a flat. No stairs. We can take it slow, I have two bedrooms. Start as roommates. No pressure, but the offer is out there. I promise to behave myself."

Esme considered this, realizing she was running out of options. Her time was up at the halfway house, her apartment was gone. She'd need help getting around for some time, and the hospital was pushing her release to free up the bed. As promised, Becky and Mario had covered her bills, however, the hospital needed the space. Esme chewed her lip and nodded. She wrote down her reply.

"Okay, but not as roommates. That would be weird, and I don't think we could stick to that. I'll move in with you, and we can live together. As a couple."

Pete blushed and smiled as he read the words she'd scribbled on the paper. Even though they hadn't consummated their relationship, they were deeply drawn to each other. "I like you, Esme. I want you to move in."

The rest of his visit, they watched terrible game shows and held hands. Pete checked the time and got up. "Damn. Sorry, I need to get to work. I'd stay here all day if I could. When do they expect to release you?"

Esme took the pad of paper and wrote a response. "As soon as they can. They said I'd be good to leave once I could open my eyes. So here we are. I can't walk on my own, though. I need crutches at least, maybe a wheelchair."

Pete's face was hard to read as he scanned her words. He rubbed his bottom lip and pushed his glasses up on his nose. "Alright, let me see what I can do. I'll be back tomorrow, okay? I'll let the doctors know you are coming home with me and see what they say. Esme?"

She stared at him, her head tilted, waiting for him to go on. Pete's face turned bright red, and he looked away. Just when she thought he wasn't going to say anything else to her, he took the pad of paper and wrote something down. He folded it and tucked it in her hand, meeting her eyes.

Esme frowned as he leaned over and kissed her forehead. He went to the door and turned around with a smile, the lines in his face making her feel giddy. After he left, she unfolded the note and read it, tears springing to her eyes.

"I love you," the note said.

No one had ever loved Esme like Pete did. Becky loved her like family. Aunt Darla, too. She hadn't remembered her father as more than a tall shadow passing through. Her mother not at all. She was an image in photos Esme couldn't connect to. Pete, though, had become a large part of her world and made her feel things she didn't think possible.

As she ran her fingers over the note, Felicia came in with a scowl on her petite, pointy face. She glanced at Esme as she flopped on her bed with a dramatic groan. "That physical therapist is sadistic."

Esme put her hands in the air as if to ask why, and Felicia pushed her thin blond hair out of her face. "Not really, but he doesn't listen when I say I can't do something. He makes me try even when I don't want to. He's kinda cute, though."

Esme smiled. She'd seen the physical therapist when he came to the room for Felicia. He was cute, but not like Pete. Felicia changed the channel to a soap opera and glazed out in front of the screen until she dozed off.

Esme fell asleep, as well, and was woken up by a nurse bringing her dinner. Jello, mashed potatoes, soup. It was the first food she'd been brought and had been getting sustenance through a feed tube because of the damage to her throat. She stared at the food in concern. She'd been sipping water, but food was a whole other issue. The tray of benign food caused real panic in her.

The nurse shook her head. "The doctor just wants you to try and see if you can swallow food. You have been getting water to pass through; try a few bites. If you can't swallow, we need to know before you get discharged."

Esme waited for the nurse to leave and poked the jello with a spoon. Terror washed over her as she thought about choking. What if she tried to swallow and the food got stuck, cutting off her airway? Her chest tightened at the memory of suffocating after the accident. She pushed the tray away and bit back tears.

"Soup is pretty much liquid," Felicia said from across the room. "Start with that."

Esme glanced down at the soup. It was basically only broth with a few floating carrot and celery slivers. Esme scooped a small amount and placed it in her mouth. She let it trickle down her throat like she did with water and swallowed. No problem. She did this a few more times, gaining confidence. Next, she took a tiny amount of Jell-O and did the same thing. It slid down no problem. It felt weird, moving past the damaged tissue, but it dissolved quickly.

Last, Esme tried the mashed potatoes, but as soon as the thicker substance hit her throat, fear took over. She began to gag and try to cough it up. Coughing hurt like hell, and tears ran down her cheeks from the pain. Finally, she swallowed, and the paste-like goo slid past the lump in her throat. However, one spoonful was enough, and she shoved the rest away.

"See? Not so bad," Felicia encouraged her from her bed. "Tomorrow will be even better. Maybe you'll even be able to talk a little."

They watched television until it was dark, and Esme rolled over to face the wall. She had so many questions she wanted to ask Felicia, but no way to do it. They'd tried passing notes, but that meant Felicia had to keep getting out of bed to bring notes back and forth, and that made Esme feel guilty. So she stopped writing back, and Felicia seemed to forget about it.

It was better that way, anyway. Soon they'd both be released to their lives, and Esme doubted they'd ever speak again. Life was like that. People came and went, rarely ever stayed. Esme would go onto her life with Pete, and Felicia would go... Esme realized she knew literally nothing about the girl in the room with her. Other than her age, name, and favorite things. Even their notes were nothing more than talking about hospital staff or music and books.

Did Felicia have family? No one had come to see her that Esme knew of, but she'd just started being able to see again, so maybe they had. Then again, she was listening to everything. She hadn't heard anyone other than staff come in and speak to Felicia. This made her sad, and she thought she should invite Felicia over once they were both out of the hospital. Maybe like her, Felicia didn't have anyone. Esme at least had Pete.

Esme set her mind to communicate with Felicia in the morning, so they could exchange contact information before she was released. She'd need to give Pete's number since she would be living there. Maybe she and Felicia could become friends. She'd never really had a friend outside of Pete and... No, just Pete.

Marty wasn't real.

The next morning, Esme woke up determined to learn more about Felicia and connect with her. She sat up, her eyes clearer than the day before. She tried speaking, but nothing came out except a low hiss. Her eyes shifted to Felicia's bed, and her heart began to race. The bed was empty and made up. Nothing around the space was personal, and the television was off in the corner.

Felicia was gone.

Chapter Twenty-Three

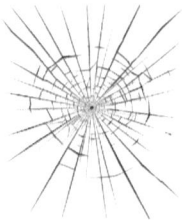

The next ten years passed without any extraordinary incident. Unlike the individual moments of Esme's childhood, riddled with traumatic events, this time was uneventful. Esme healed in Pete's home, and over time, it became hers, as well. Her voice never fully recovered, but she could speak in a low whisper for short bursts before her voice tired and faded out. After a couple of years of living together, Pete and Esme tied the knot, with Jo and Linda as witnesses at the courthouse, and went about their lives like always. Esme figured the strange visitors from her past were gone and something she could pack away like a photo album.

She hoped.

Esme finished her schooling to become a veterinarian technician but put her dreams on hold to become a veterinarian because she found the school workload to be too much for her healing body and strained voice. Even so, she found a job at a local veterinarian clinic and worked diligently to help every animal she came across. It broke her heart every time one died.

Pete ended up managing Mama Jo's pizza when Jo and Linda decided to hit the road and travel for their golden years. Between both of their jobs, Pete and Esme had a comfortable little life and eventually bought a cute, quaint home in a small subdivision.

Esme didn't have any unexpected visitors over the years, at least ones she wasn't sure were real. Sometimes she'd find herself chatting with a random stranger at work or in the grocery store, and the old fear would come up. Were they really there, or was she imagining them? However, nothing out of the ordinary struck her, and she was happy to put her tumultuous childhood behind her.

Becky reached out now and then, sent cards and photos of her little family. They had another child, a boy, and their holiday card picture always seemed too perfect to Esme. She often found herself scanning their faces, trying to uncover an untold secret. Somewhat disappointed, she found she could never detect one. Not sure why she wanted Becky to fail on some level, guilt kept Esme from allowing them to reform a connection as family. Becky was better off without her.

When Esme and Pete turned thirty, they discussed the possibility of having children of their own. Esme was vehemently opposed to the idea due to her own terrible childhood, and Pete, although somewhat disappointed, agreed their own traumatic upbringings were reason enough to skip introducing children into the world.

Esme could never get over how deeply Pete loved her. He surprised her with flowers and little quirky gifts all the time, her favorite kind. She couldn't shake the feeling that one day she would wake up and he'd simply be gone like everyone else in her life. His side of the bed would be cold as if he'd never slept there. Yet, every morning, there he was resting beside her, his face happy and peaceful.

Shortly after turning thirty-three, Esme found herself exhausted beyond belief and barely able to make it through a work shift. After a couple of months of that, she finally buckled and made an appointment with a doctor to get some bloodwork done. She hated doctors and didn't trust them. However, Pete was worried and insisted she at least get an examination.

Sitting in the sterile doctor's office, Esme fought back fear, convinced they were going to take her back to the mental hospital. *A mistake,* they'd say, *you were never supposed to leave.* When the doctor walked in, however, her face was calm and reassuring.

"Hello, Esme, I am Dr. Walker. We ran your blood tests, and everything looks good, nothing to be concerned about. Your iron is a little low, but a supplement should take care of that. Were you and your husband trying to conceive?" she asked, glancing at the chart in her hands.

"Conceive what?" Esme replied, confused.

Pete, who was sitting on a stool across the room, tipped his head. "A baby?"

Dr. Walker smiled. "Yes, a baby. Esme, you are almost three months along, which could explain your exhaustion. When was your last cycle?"

Esme frowned. She had no idea. They always used birth control, and her days ran into one another. "I don't remember. They never have been terribly regular."

"Well, I'm guessing somewhere around four months ago," Dr. Walker said, then glanced at Esme. She turned to Pete. "Would you mind waiting outside, so I can go over something with Esme?"

Pete rose and furrowed his brow as worry crossed his face. "Is everything alright?"

Dr. Walker smiled. "Yes, I simply need to meet with my patient alone for legal reasons."

Pete looked unsure, but Esme nodded to let him know she was alright. He slipped out of the room, shutting the door quietly behind him with a glance back at Esme. Dr. Walker turned to Esme once they were alone and set the chart down, meeting her eyes.

"I take it this isn't welcome news?" she asked.

Esme fought back tears. She loved Pete more than anything, but they'd agreed not to have children. She couldn't be a mother; she could hardly be herself. "No."

Dr Walker gazed at the door, then back. "Are you in any danger?"

"No! It's not that. I... I'm just not meant to be a mom," Esme confessed.

"I see. Well, there are options for an unwanted pregnancy. Would you like me to go over them with you?"

Esme shook her head. "I need to think. This is all completely out of the blue. Not what I was expecting when I came in today. How much time do I have to decide?"

Dr. Walker grimaced. "Not much legally. After three months along, your options are greatly limited by law. I'd recommend you make a decision in the next week or so."

A week? Esme had just found out her body was being invaded; now she was under pressure to decide what to do about it within a week. Plus, there was Pete. Despite what he said, he might have feelings about having the baby. Esme wanted to cry.

"Thank you. Can I go now? I don't feel so well."

"Of course. Here is my card. Please contact me as soon as you can about what you decide to do. No judgment here, I simply want you to be safe," Dr. Walker handed Esme a business card and jotted down a couple of notes in the chart.

Esme left the office and found Pete leaning against a wall in the hallway leading to the elevator. His face was white as a sheet, and he appeared like he'd been crying. Esme took his extended hand and they walked in silence to the elevator. The ride home was quiet, though Pete tried to make small talk. Esme was recoiling from the thought of something growing inside her. Taking her over.

Once home, they each found tasks to keep them busy, and by the time the tiny home was spotless, they sat down to eat together. Pete reached out and covered Esme's hand with his own, his eyes sincere.

"I know we didn't expect this, but could it be a good thing? Maybe we can undo our own childhoods and give this child the life we deserved?" he asked.

Esme met his eyes, seeing a little glimmer of hope in them. A glimmer she couldn't return. She tried to smile to reassure him, but felt like her face made a monstrous expression instead. Pete didn't seem to notice, however, his eyes grew concerned. He squeezed her hand.

"If you don't want this child, I understand and I support whatever decision you need to make. We agreed not to have children, but clearly the universe had other plans. I won't lie and say part of me is wanting to be a father, but we need to be in this together. I would never ask you to do something you didn't want to do."

Esme appreciated his consideration, but now knew she couldn't get rid of the child. His confession made her realize no matter what, things *had* changed. If she chose to terminate the pregnancy, he'd still love her, but part of who they were would die at that moment. She glanced at her stomach and gritted her teeth as she made the decision.

"The doctor says I'm too far along to terminate," she lied, giving Pete an out of making him think he was forcing her to carry the baby.

"What about adoption?" he asked, also giving her an out to raising a child.

Adoption. Esme let her mind run over that possibility. However, she knew once they saw the baby, they wouldn't be able to give it to complete strangers. Despite their desire to be childfree, the idea of trusting anyone else with such a fragile being was outside of their nature.

Esme shook her head, feeling overwhelmed. "I'm tired, Pete. Can we not talk about this tonight? I think our only choice is to have the baby and see what happens. Maybe it won't be as bad as we think."

Pete tried to read her face, then kissed her fingers. "I'm here for you, Esme."

He was. It wasn't enough. Esme excused herself to bed, and Pete came to lie with her for a bit. Not wanting to hurt him but needing time to herself to absorb her new reality, she turned away from him. Pete touched her back, then left to go read in the living room.

Esme lay in bed, running her fingers across where she assumed the baby was growing, and wept silently. Eventually, she tired herself out and dozed off. A little while later, she felt Pete climb into bed and rolled over to put her arm around him as an apology for shutting him out earlier.

Something was off.

She opened her eyes and tried to focus in the dark. His skin felt cold, rough. She ran her hands down his arm and jerked back when she got to the long, pointed nails. It wasn't *Pete* in bed beside her.

Her hand fumbled for the bedside lamp, and she stifled a scream when the lamp cast its light on the shape in the bed. A cackle rose into the air, and Esme clambered out of the bed, terrified at the sight before her.

The creature rose from the bed, its long arms dragging across the bedspread. Long, stringy, red hair hung from the weathered, broad face, and neon green eyes locked onto Esme's as it crawled across the bed toward her. Esme pressed herself against the wall, trying to convince herself she was simply having a nightmare.

A recurring nightmare from years before.

It was only stress, that was all. She simply needed to wake herself up to end what was happening. Pinching her arm as hard as she could, Esme closed her eyes and reopened them, hoping to come out of the nightmare.

Nothing changed. It was still there.

This isn't real, Esme told herself as she attempted to create as much space as she could between herself and her old companion.

"Baby," Lamia hissed as she reached out and covered Esme's belly with her wrinkled, clammy hand.

Chapter Twenty-Four

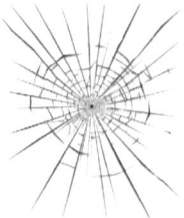

T he scream that erupted from Esme's chest broke through scar tissue in her throat. Pete came running into the room, his eyes frantic and his fists balled up to fight the unknown assailant. The door rattled on its hinges as he flung it open, scanning the room for the threat. Instead, he found Esme trembling against the wall, her hands protectively in front of her.

Thinking her scream and hands had to do with the baby, he rushed over and took her hands in his, his eyes searching her face. "Are you alright? Is the baby okay?"

The word *baby* set her off, and she began to scream again, shoving him away as she formed herself into a ball against the wall. "She's back! I can't. I can't do this!"

Pete frowned, confused by her words. "She? The baby? What are you talking about, Esme? Who's back?"

Lamia crouched on the bed behind Pete, drool dripping from her large, twisted mouth as if she was ready to feast. She waved her hands in the air, making Esme think about the chorus kids in school with their white gloves and jazz hands. The creature knew exactly what she was doing and was making her presence known. Yes, Lamia was back, but this Lamia was different... sinister.

Lamia always had a dark streak in her, but generally only shadowed Esme. Well, until Allison. Esme truly believed Lamia had something to do with Allison's death. Suicide, they said, however, Esme felt it was something more to it. Lamia had gotten into Allison's head somehow. Of this, Esme had no doubt, even though she had no way to prove it.

Lamia cocked her head, and her face changed in the blink of an eye. Esme saw something in the creature that made her shudder. In a matter of seconds, Lamia's face contorted to show Esme Gogo, Tall Man, Marty, and a series of faces she didn't recognize. Then it settled back to Lamia's large, wrinkly face. The creature cackled.

"Baby."

What did that mean? Was Lamia a culmination of all of Esme's companions? Or was she showing Esme, she knew about them? That they weren't truly gone. What did any of this have to do with the baby growing inside her? Esme turned her eyes away from Lamia and focused on Pete.

"I think I'm losing my mind, Pete," she whispered, ignoring the dancing creature trying to get her attention. It was the first time she'd said the words out loud, but had been aware for years she was always on the precipice of insanity. All the years of peace were only a veil, hiding the monstrosities behind, waiting to reappear and take their rightful place in Esme's mind.

Pete gathered her in his arms and kissed the side of her head. "No, Esme, you are dealing with a lot. Finding out about the pregnancy was a shock to both of us. You need some rest. Do you want me to make something to eat?" Pete offered, rubbing her back.

The idea of food turned her stomach, but Lamia happily taunting them from the bed was getting to be too much at the moment. Esme nodded.

"That sounds nice. I'll help."

Pete smiled and took her hand. "No, let me cook for you, but come give me something pretty to look at in the kitchen while I do."

Esme wanted to protest, but Pete clearly wanted to take care of her. They went to the door, and Esme paused. "I'll be there in a minute."

Pete watched her for a moment to make sure she was okay, then grinned. "I'll be waiting."

He went to the kitchen, and she could hear him putting pans on the stove. She whipped around, her eyes blazing, and stared at Lamia. Lamia stopped her weird side-to-side movements and tipped her head at Esme, her eyes registering insecurity.

Esme stepped forward. "You will not mess this up for me. Pete is everything to me, do you understand? I don't want or need you around. Your time with me is over."

Lamia gazed at her placidly, then roared with laughter. The sound reverberated through the room. As she shook her enormous head, it reminded Esme of the puppets she'd watch on television when she was a child. Lamia moved like a giant puppet, but who was controlling the strings?

Lamia climbed off the bed too fluidly for her size. Almost like she *slithered*. Esme took an involuntary step back as Lamia moved toward her. The serpentine creature hovered over Esme, who stood her ground. Lamia leaned down and hissed in Esme's ear.

"Baby."

That was it. Lamia came back because of the baby. Now, not only was Esme stuck with an unwanted pregnancy, she was tormented by a monster from her past because of it. As long as she was pregnant or had the baby in her life, Lamia wouldn't let her be.

Esme shoved past the creature and hurried out the door to the kitchen, praying Lamia wouldn't follow her. Pete was leaning over the stove, peering into a pot.

He turned and smiled when she came in. "There she is. Pasta Florentine sound good? I can make some garlic bread to go with it."

Esme sat on a stool at a short counter sticking out from the wall. "Sounds wonderful. Pete, um, I think I need to talk to the doctor about the pregnancy."

"Oh, is everything alright? Did something happen you are worried about?"

If he meant something by the fact Esme was being stalked by a creepy puppet who was obsessed with the baby, then, yes. "No, I'm just having second thoughts."

Pete paused and leaned against the counter, his eyes concerned. "I see. I thought you said it was too late for us to, well, you know?"

She had told him that. Damnit. She shrugged. "I guess, but I thought I'd talk to her, anyway, and see what my options are. I'm feeling really out of sorts about all of this."

"What about adoption?" Pete asked. "Like an open adoption where we can still stay in touch?"

Esme stared at her husband and could see his pain. He was doing his best to support her decision, but he was already invested since she told him they were having the baby. Besides, if they put the child up for adoption, Esme feared Lamia wouldn't let it go.

What if she haunted the child, too?

"I'm sorry, Pete, I'm all over the place right now," Esme confessed. "Let me sleep on it."

"Of course, I'm here if you need to talk. We are in this together," Pete replied gently.

She knew he was, and it made it that much harder. He didn't deserve any of this. He deserved the simple little family he worked so hard to create. Esme smiled her appreciation for him, and he rotated to pour pasta into the boiling water.

The doctor said she had a week to decide. What if she went forward with terminating the pregnancy, then told Pete she lost the baby? He would still feel bad but think it was out of their control. It was the kindest way to let him down, Esme believed. As if reading her thoughts, Lamia appeared in the kitchen doorway, her eyes glowing.

"Our baby," she said through her sharp teeth.

Lamia believed the baby was hers, as well. That could be a problem. Esme frowned at the creature and mentally told Lamia to leave her alone. This agitated Lamia, who began dragging her nails along the kitchen walls. Esme glanced at Pete, who was focused on making a homemade sauce. He was unaware of the monster hovering in there with them.

Of course he was. Like all the other companions before, no one but Esme could see or interact with them. Sort of. Lamia clearly found ways to push through the veil. Speaking of, the creature was now standing right behind Pete, breathing down his neck. He instinctively touched the pack of his neck, and Esme cringed. Whether or not he could see Lamia, part of him was aware of her presence.

Esme set her mind to her plan. Go one day when Pete was at work and terminate the pregnancy, then tell him she miscarried. This would get Lamia out of their life once and for all. Esme hoped. Pete finished making dinner and served Esme a plate as he sat down across from her. She smiled at the one person who mattered to her.

"Thanks, Pete. It smells wonderful."

"Anything for you, babe."

The following morning, after Pete left for work, Esme decided to go to a clinic across town, not affiliated with her doctor. She knew if she went through her doctor, Pete would find out. She called and they agreed to see her as soon as possible. Taking the bus, so she had the car for errands, Pete kissed her and strolled out the door to the bus stop.

Once she was sure he was gone. Esme loaded up in the car and headed out, going the opposite direction of his job. She eased the car out of the neighborhood and gripped the steering wheel with both hands. Guilt racked her, and she silently apologized to the baby and Pete. She needed to do this; it was the only way to be free. To be safe.

On the way to the clinic, a woman standing on the side of the road caught Esme's attention, and she lost her focus on the road for a moment. Felicia? The blond woman standing on the side of the road had dark skin, light hair, and green eyes that were so striking. Esme pulled her foot off the gas, her eyes locked on the slim figure. Older, but the same. The woman turned her attention to Esme's vehicle as a huge smile broke out across her face.

It was Felicia.

Esme shook her head. Was she real? Had she ever been? Felicia went to raise her hand in a wave, then frowned and began frantically pointing. Esme followed the gesture and saw an old man crossing the road in front of her. She slammed on the brakes and jerked the wheel to avoid him. The motion caused the vehicle to career sideways and flip over, rolling multiple times. Esme lost consciousness on the second roll.

Hands pulling her from the vehicle brought her back to consciousness, and she peered up into the eyes of the paramedics rescuing her. One of them turned back to someone behind them. "She's awake!"

Esme was relatively unscathed, considering the car was a crumpled mess. Bruised and shaken up, but otherwise uninjured. "What happened?"

"Witnesses said you swerved to avoid a pedestrian, and the car rolled. We're taking you in for observation. What is your name?"

"Esme."

"Okay, Esme, we are about to move you to the ambulance to take you to the hospital."

"No, I'm okay. Was one of the witnesses a blond woman named Felicia?" Esme asked, scanning the crowd for Felicia. She didn't see her.

"I can't say. The police are talking to witnesses. We need to at least take you in for scans and X-rays. You can leave after that if you feel up to it."

Esme sighed. "Fine."

"Can we call someone for you?" the paramedic asked.

Pete? He was going to be so worried. Esme considered not telling them to contact him, but knew he'd find out anyway. "My husband."

They took his information, and one of them left to call him at work. When they came back, the paramedic who called was pale, his eyes wide. He whispered to the other paramedic, who turned to Esme.

"You are pregnant?"

Esme nodded. There was no way out of it now. Lamia was getting what she wanted. In her mind, Esme could hear Lamia's cackle as she hissed, "Our baby."

Chapter Twenty-Five

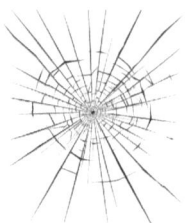

"**B**reathe. In, out, take your time," the midwife instructed, bracing Esme so she could lean back.

Esme rested against the sweat-drenched pillows. Like it or not, this baby was coming. Pete was by her side, wiping her brow between contractions. While she was grateful for his attentive nature, she wanted this all to be over with. To face the baby on the outside and figure out what to do.

Over the last six months, Lamia had become more aggressive toward Esme, as if she was punishing her for having a baby. Sometimes, Esme would wake up with bruises and scratches she couldn't recall getting and knew they were a result of Lamia's resentment toward her.

Lamia hovered constantly, however, one thing Esme noted was that Lamia made herself scarce when Pete was around. This made Esme unusually clingy when Pete was home, but he didn't seem to mind. He'd always been the more physical one of the two of them, and he was enjoying Esme's need to be close, even though he didn't understand the change in her. Another change pregnancy brought was all.

Another contraction surged through her body, and Esme grimaced with the pain. She wished she was more excited about the end result, but that too seemed like an invasion of sorts. She didn't want to be a mother. Pete, on the other hand, had grown more used to the idea and painted a room to be a nursery and began bringing home little gifts for the baby. Jo and Linda had done a silent shower for the impending child, not requiring Esme to be on show.

Esme had never heard the term, but Jo assured her it would be a great way to get starter items for the baby. So she arranged everything, and on a set day, baby gifts began arriving at their house. Even food and things for Esme. She and Pete were able to open the gifts at their leisure and kept track of the gift givers. No weird party games, no awkward small talk. Esme was grateful for Jo's thoughtfulness both in gathering gifts for the baby and also respecting Esme's desire not to be a party trick.

After the silent shower, Esme began to warm up to the idea of the baby about to join them. Or so she thought. After Pete left for work one morning, she went to shower, avoiding looking at her odd-shaped belly in the mirror. The hot water loosened her lower back as she sighed. She couldn't wait to have her body back.

Once the hot water ran out, Esme cut the shower off and wrapped herself in a large, fluffy towel. She'd bought oversized towels as her body grew, and was grateful for the extra material to hide her strange-shaped body. She padded down the hall to her room, passing by the nursery.

Movement in the room caught her eye, and she paused, catching her breath. A shadow crossed in front of the large windows. Lamia. What was she doing in there?

Esme clicked the overhead light on and gasped. Baby clothes and items were strewn all around the room. Packages of diapers had been ripped open, and more than one pastel stuffed animal was torn apart, soft white fluff tossed everywhere.

Esme glared at Lamia, who was standing sheepishly off to the side. "What have you done?"

Lamia hung her head, but Esme knew the creature wasn't sorry for what she had done. Lamia was playing a game. Esme began to scoop up the stuffed animal insides with one hand as she clutched the towel closed with the other. The white stuffing stuck to her hand and gave her the sensation of cotton candy. She gagged and dropped it in an elephant-shaped trash can. Wild animals was the nursery theme, but as Esme continued to pick up dismembered baby toys, she thought it should be slaughterhouse themed. This almost made her laugh, but Lamia was making an odd sound in the corner.

What was she doing?

Lamia opened her mouth wide, her yellowed fangs filling the space. She let out a strange catlike sound, a screech. She did it again, staring at Esme for some kind of validation. That's when it dawned on Esme what Lamia was doing. She was mimicking a baby's cry. A shudder ran through Esme as she recognized how close to real it was. Where would Lamia have heard a baby cry?

After cleaning up the room and discarding anything not salvageable, Esme knew she needed to create a buffer between her and Lamia. Pete wasn't enough anymore. She needed something while he was gone from home. Something Lamia wouldn't like.

What that was, Esme didn't know.

By the time Pete got home that night, the nursery didn't appear as if anything happened in there. They watched television, and Pete rubbed Esme's swollen ankles.

"Not much longer," he said and stroked her leg.

Esme smiled but pushed down the worry. As much as she wanted her body back, the idea of another being to take care of was terrifying. Even so, she didn't want to let Pete down. He got up to get them each a cup of tea, and Esme glanced around the room. This was usually when Lamia showed up. The room remained empty. Esme took stock of the room, trying to see what might be different.

The television droned on, but everything else seemed the same. Then, Esme noticed Pete had lit candles on the mantle. She thought back to any time she saw Lamia and if candles had ever been burning. Not that she could think of. The candles were soy; Pete insisted on those because they burned cleaner. He didn't want Esme or the baby being exposed to unnecessary chemicals.

Pete came back in and handed Esme a cup of tea with a kiss on the top of her head. They finished the tea and headed to bed, Pete helping Esme get up off the couch. Esme grabbed a candle on her way out of the room and carried it to their bedroom.

When Pete left the next morning, Esme lit the candle and waited. No Lamia. She went from room to room with the candle and didn't see the creature. Was that all it took? Deciding she needed to know for sure, she blew out the candle once she was in the kitchen.

The sound of scratching behind her made Esme jump, and she turned around to see Lamia standing in the shadows, her eyes angry. She knew what Esme was doing, using the lit candle to keep her away. Esme tried to light the candle, and Lamia charged her, knocking Esme over.

Esme braced herself as she fell, protecting her stomach despite her feelings about becoming a mother. Lamia hovered over her, breathing heavily. Esme reached out for the candle, but Lamia kicked it out of the way. Esme crawled across the floor toward the candle. Lamia beat her to it and put a wall between Esme and her goal.

Esme rolled over and sat up, knowing she was beat. "Fine, you win, Lamia."

The creature seemed unsure but backed off, even so. Esme left the candle on the floor, determined to get it once Lamia forgot about it. She stumbled to her feet and pretended to get busy making food, ignoring the creature. Lamia rocked side to side, watching Esme.

When Pete got home and found the candle in the middle of the floor, he frowned and scooped it up. He set it on the counter and went to check on Esme, who was napping. She felt him climb in beside her and wrap his arm around her. She rolled over to face him, relieved he was home. "How was your day?" she murmured into his chest.

"Good. Busy. Hey, there was a candle in the middle of the kitchen floor?"

Esme blinked up at him. "Oh yeah. I was trying to light it and dropped it. My stomach got in the way of picking it up. Sorry."

Pete laughed. "No need to apologize. Tell you what. I will put candles in every room of the house where you can light them. That way, you don't need to carry them around with you. Deal?"

"Deal," Esme agreed, knowing this would help keep Lamia at bay.

Pete did as promised, and Esme lit candles as she moved from room to room when he wasn't home. As suspected, Lamia became scarce. Sometimes, Esme would hear the creature hissing or scratching nails in another room, but didn't see her. The rest of her pregnancy went without incident.

So the morning Esme climbed out of bed to see Pete off to work and water gushed between her legs, it took her by surprise. She and Pete stared at each other as a puddle formed on the floor at her feet. Pete's eyes grew wide, and he ran to the closet to grab the bag they'd packed for the occasion.

"Is this it?" he asked, scoping the floral printed bag up with one hand.

"Yes, that's the one," Esme replied, trying to slip her shoes on.

Then the first real contraction hit, and she doubled over. "This is it."

They rushed to the hospital and met the midwife when they arrived. Esme was prepped and brought into a birthing room. Pete went with a hospital worker to fill out insurance paperwork.

Once Esme was in the room and settled into the bed, she was left alone for a moment. She closed her eyes as another contraction hit, wishing Pete would hurry back. She was scared and needed him near. That's when she heard it.

The hiss.

Esme opened her eyes and saw Lamia standing in the corner. The creature appeared larger, more angry. Her bright green eyes were fixed on Esme as spittle dripped from her teeth. She lifted her long arm and stretched out her sharp fingernails, pointing at Esme.

"My baby," she said.

Esme shuddered. Lamia had called it "baby" and "our baby" but never "my baby." Esme knew the change wasn't good. Lamia was angry Esme had kept her away and wanted vengeance. Now she was in the way of the creature getting what she wanted.

"Please, Pete, hurry up," she whispered.

Lamia came closer, a twisted grin on her face as she reached out for Esme's belly. At that moment, the door flew open and Pete rushed in, his eyes worried. He came to her side, grabbing her hand in his.

"I'm sorry it took so long, Esme. Too much paperwork. Are you alright?"

A contraction surged over her, and she groaned. Pete leaned next to her, holding her hand in his as she squeezed it. The pain kept her from speaking until it eased between contractions. However, Lamia was no longer there. This made Esme uneasy as it was easier to know what Lamia was up to when she could keep eyes on the creature.

The midwife came in with a nurse after a few minutes and checked Esme. She nodded and sat down. "You are already seven centimeters dilated. Not much longer now. Try to rest between contractions because you are going to need your energy to push when it comes time."

Esme glanced at Pete, fear in her eyes. He leaned close and whispered, "We got this. I'm right here."

For some reason, that helped, and the labor progressed at lightning speed. When it came time to push, it was as if Esme's body was on autopilot. Even if she didn't want to, her body knew exactly what to do to bring the baby forth. Her muscles jumped in, and her whole body became a machine to force the baby out.

"Alright, keep pushing," the midwife instructed. "I can see the head!"

Esme leaned forward and pushed with all of her might, feeling her body seem to split in two. The pain and pressure were immense. She felt the head pop out and the midwife ease the rest of the baby's body through.

"It's a girl!" the midwife exclaimed, holding the red and squirming baby up to show them their daughter.

"A girl," Pete whispered, his eyes wide with astonishment. He reached out and placed his hand on the baby's small head. "Our child."

Esme glanced at her daughter, not finding connection. The midwife warned her that it was common and not to worry about it. Bonding takes time, she'd told Esme. Even so, Esme was hoping she would feel something for the baby. Then she heard it. A sound she hoped she wouldn't. One she dreaded.

Lamia cackled all around her.

Chapter Twenty-Six

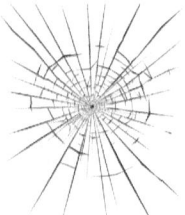

Something about the baby's birth brought Lamia to the forefront, breaking the barriers that were previously keeping her at bay. She showed up when Pete was around, and candles no longer kept her away. It was as if she was directly tied to the baby's presence and was able to cross boundaries because of it.

As for the baby, they named her Elizabeth after Pete's grandmother and called her Lizzy, since his grandmother went by Beth. Pete was smitten with the tiny, dark-haired child. Esme, on the other hand, still couldn't connect to the tiny child. She was diligent at the everyday tasks of caring for her daughter, such as feeding, bathing, and holding. However, it all seemed functional. She was committed to protecting Lizzy, but out of a sense of responsibility versus love.

Lamia hovered constantly, but not in a nurturing way. She almost seemed agitated by Lizzy's existence, her baby demands on Esme. Lamia shifted side to side and made a strange grumbling sound in her throat whenever Lizzy was near. It was disconcerting, but Esme tried to stay focused on Lizzy's care and not play into Lamia's drama.

Pete didn't want to leave to go back to work. Even though Jo gave him a decent amount of time off after the baby was born, bills began to pile up. With Esme not working and the added expense of a child, they were barely scraping by. So Pete went to work and rushed home as soon as he was off. Esme was grateful for him, as he immediately took Lizzy off her hands as soon as he was home to give her a break. She looked forward to that time every day and counted the hours until Pete returned.

After a couple of months, Esme began to worry she would never connect to her daughter and began to look into what was going on with her. The midwife said it was likely postpartum depression and recommended tips to help Esme bridge the gap. However, some of her old personality traits came back through, and she found herself losing periods of time. Afraid she'd worry Pete, she didn't tell him what was going on with her.

One day, after he left for work, she lay Lizzy down for a nap and went to the kitchen to make a cup of tea. At least Lizzy was an easy baby and napped often. Esme put the kettle on and opened a book to read while it heated. A wave of exhaustion came over her, and she shut the book, closing her eyes with her head on the table until the kettle went off.

She woke up to the house filled with smoke and Lizzy wailing from her crib. Esme jumped up, confused, and glanced around the kitchen. The kettle was red hot and smoking. She ran to the stove and cut the burner off, shifting the now-empty kettle to another burner. The water was completely gone, and a look at the clock showed she'd fallen asleep for over thirty minutes. Even the screaming kettle and crying baby had failed to wake her up.

Lizzy was hysterical, and Esme shoved windows open before grabbing the baby. The smoke had spread through the whole house, and Esme realized she could have burned it down. She went to Lizzy's nursery and pushed open the door, shutting it behind her to hopefully prevent the smoke from coming in.

A shadow moved near the crib, and Esme saw Lamia hovering over the baby. The creature seemed more agitated than usual and was hissing and drooling as she did her odd dance side to side.

"Get away from her," Esme ordered.

Lamia met her eyes with a strange grin and reached her long nail toward the baby in rebellion to Esme's demand. Shocking Esme, the nail cut the baby's cheek, causing Lizzy to wail even louder. Esme ran to the crib and snatched the baby up, cradling her close.

"Don't you dare touch her again," Esme yelled, causing Lizzy to jerk in her arms.

Lamia laughed, her drool dripping down to the crib sheets. She leaned close to Esme. "Touch her again."

Even though it seemed like Lamia was mimicking her, Esme knew better. It was a threat. She turned the baby away from the creature and ran out of the room. There was no point, however. Lamia could follow her anywhere and wasn't going to give up that easily. Esme was going to have to make sure Lamia was never left alone with the baby.

She sliced Lizzy's cheek.

That revelation scared the hell out of Esme. Lamia was becoming stronger, able to cross boundaries she couldn't before. Esme didn't feel connected to her child, but she didn't want any harm to befall the innocent baby.

When Pete got home and picked Lizzy up, Esme decided to broach the subject. "I think we should move Lizzy into our room at night."

Pete frowned, then made a silly face at his daughter. "Okay. Any reason why?"

Esme glanced at the scratch. "She was napping and somehow got that scratch on her cheek. I'd just feel better if we could keep an eye on her around the clock. At least until she's a little older."

"You don't have to convince me," Pete said, kissing the baby's soft head. "I'd bring her with me to work if they'd allow it. I miss her when I'm gone."

Esme smiled. She knew he would. Even though she was struggling with motherhood, she admired Pete's utter devotion to both Lizzy and her. She went to take a shower while Pete had Lizzy and cried as the hot water cascaded down her skin. She wanted to bond with her daughter, she didn't know how. Sometimes she felt a pang of something when she saw Pete with Lizzy. Not jealousy, but something close to it. Feeling left out, maybe.

After her shower, she went to their bedroom and sat on the edge of the bed. She could hear Pete making goofy sounds at Lizzy and the baby gurgling in return. Esme wiped her nose on the towel and slipped on pajamas. She knew she'd let things slip since having the baby, but it was barely enough to make it through the day.

Pete was in the kitchen when she came down, holding Lizzy in one arm and making stew with the other. He was such a natural at being a father; it made Esme feel incompetent. He winked at her.

"Heating up some stew and biscuits. Why don't you hang out for a bit?"

"Do you want me to take the baby?" she asked.

Pete grinned at Lizzy. "No, she's helping me cook."

Esme laughed. Pete had that effect on her. He was always so calm and satisfied with everything. Esme sat on a stool and watched him. "How was work?"

"Good. Jo says hello. She actually brought something up to me today, and I wanted to talk to you about it," Pete replied as he bounced Lizzy with his arm.

"Oh? What's that?" For some reason, alarm bells went off in Esme.

"She is ready to retire. She asked if I wanted to buy the restaurant. I told her I would talk to you about it."

Esme frowned. They didn't have the money to buy a restaurant. "I don't understand. With what money?"

Pete turned off the stove top. Lizzy had fallen asleep in his arms. "Hold on, let me lay her down."

He left the room and placed Lizzy in a bassinet in the living room. Esme noticed Lamia in the corner, and a warning went off in her head. "Bring the bassinet in here, so we can keep an eye on her while we eat."

Lamia hissed at Esme as Pete carried the bassinet in. He placed Lizzy by the table and grabbed a couple of bowls. "Grab a seat, I'll bring you some stew."

Esme jumped up. "No, let me help, Pete. You were at work all day."

"So were you," Pete pointed out. "Let me do this for you, Esme. I love you."

She stood awkwardly, then nodded and made her way to the table. Pete brought over a bowl of stew and a biscuit on a plate. He kissed her on the head and went to get his food. Once they were sitting, he took her hand.

"Jo is willing to work with us. The payment would come out of the profits. We wouldn't need to put anything down. She and Linda are well enough off and ready to spend the rest of their days traveling. I'd be doing pretty much what I am now, and the payment would get drawn from the monthly profits."

"What if the place doesn't make money that month?" Esme asked, worried they would get buried.

"We discussed that. If a payment is missed, it will be divided over the next few months' payments. Jo really wants this for us," Pete explained.

Esme chewed her lip. "What if it starts doing badly and we can't keep up?"

Pete smiled, his eyes crinkling at the corners. "I already work there. I'd be affected if it started going badly, anyway. This allows us to be more invested in the success of the business and benefit from it."

Esme could see how badly he wanted to take the chance. She tipped her head and squeezed his hand. "I think you should do it."

"Not me. Us. This would be for our family," Pete replied, gazing at Lizzy, who was sucking on her bottom lip in her sleep.

"So what happens next?"

Pete shrugged. "We draft up a contract stating what our terms are. We won't go through a bank since this will be between us, but we will have it legally filed. Then any owner-type responsibilities will be handed to me. Jo is going to work with me for a few weeks to make sure I understand the timelines and things like that. I'd like you to be involved, too. If you want. I know this isn't your dream, but I want us to do this together as a family."

Esme considered that, then shook her head. "I really want to go back to working with animals. I'm sorry. I didn't like working there back in the day, so I'm not sure I'd like it any better now."

Pete looked disappointed but bobbed his head. "No, you're right. You are meant to work at the vet. I just want to see you more."

Esme blushed. Pete was so damn romantic. "I'll come by and have meals with you when you can't come home for dinner. Me and Lizzy. I won't be going back to work for a while as long as we can afford it while Lizzy is little. Child care is so expensive."

"So, we are doing this?" Pete asked hopefully. Lizzy began to fuss, and he scooped her up in one arm, bracing her on his shoulder.

Esme fell in love with him all over again, watching him nurture their daughter. "I think so. It seems like a smart idea. Does that make you Mama Jo, then?"

Pete laughed. "I guess so! We'll keep the name since it already has a following. Plus, I think it sounds comfortable. I can be Mama."

Esme liked how his eyes lit up talking about the restaurant. He acted like a kid on Christmas. This was clearly his journey. Pete was now Mama.

At least one of them was.

Chapter Twenty-Seven

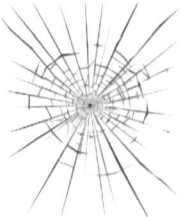

N o matter how hard she tried, Esme could never find the magical place that felt like home with Lizzy. She cared for her child and made sure all her needs were met, but even as the years passed, Esme often felt like she was watching over someone else's child.

Reality began to blur, and there were times she'd wake up and wonder not only where she was, but *who* she was. Pete was a constant lighthouse in the storm and reminded Esme where she belonged in the world. He was also a great father and made up for Esme's lack of connection to their daughter. Lizzy never seemed to notice her mother's distance and thrived in a stable and loving home.

The restaurant took off over the years, and soon they were considering opening another location. Esme went back to work when Lizzy turned three and was able to start nursery school.

She and Pete took turns dropping off and picking up their daughter, and everything appeared seamless.

However, on the night of Lizzy's fourth birthday, Esme began to sense herself slipping. She'd stopped going to therapy and taking her meds years before, not noticing much of a difference. Until now. Sure, Lamia was always present, and Esme struggled with time and space, but she could keep it together day to day. However, a shift inside Esme was happening.

That night, they put Lizzy to bed after a day of cake and presents with people they knew. The little, dark-haired girl was delighted with being four and told everyone so. Even Esme couldn't help but smile at Lizzy's joy. She was a delightful and easy-going child. It wasn't that Esme didn't want her daughter to be happy; it was that she felt like she was in the way of that. If she was honest with herself, she didn't know true happiness. She loved Pete, and being with him made her feel like she belonged, but even with him, she felt separated from herself.

They stood at the door, watching their daughter sleep, and Pete rubbed Esme's back. "She made everything whole again," he whispered.

Esme nodded, but she didn't know the feeling. "She really is something," she replied.

Pete laughed. "A mini you."

That surprised Esme as Lizzy was so full of giddiness and light. Esme felt like the dark shadow hiding in the corner. Like Lamia. Just there. Lizzy seemed to encapsulate pure energy and joy. Like Pete. "No, she's all yours."

Pete put his arms around Esme, and she leaned back into him. He kissed the back of her head. "I know we didn't plan on having children, but now that she's here, I can't imagine life without her."

Children. Surely he didn't want more? Esme let the subject drop and turned to go to the living room. "Do you want to watch something, or read for a bit?"

Pete grinned and, for a moment, looked like the young cook she met on his first day at work at the pizza place. He shook his head. "I have a better idea."

They slipped into the bedroom and took off their clothes. Pete wrapped his arms around Esme and whispered, "This is everything I ever wanted."

She could agree with that. They climbed into bed and made love, drifting off to sleep shortly after. The sound of the phone ringing woke them up in the middle of the night, and Pete groggily answered it.

"Hello? Wait, what? Slow down. Oh no, I'll be there shortly," he replied.

"What?" Esme asked, sitting up in bed.

Pete was out of bed, throwing clothes on. "Someone broke into the restaurant tonight. Trashed the place. The police are there now. I need to go speak with them and see about getting it cleaned up and secured."

"Do you want me to go with you?" Esme inquired, throwing her nightgown on.

"No, stay here with Lizzy. I need to go file a report and assess the damage. Damnit, I hope they didn't get into the safe. I didn't make the weekly deposit yet."

Esme watched Pete get ready, her heart pounding in her chest. She didn't know why, but she felt guilty about what happened. He leaned over to kiss her, his eyes filled with worry. They were just getting on their feet.

After he left, Esme couldn't sleep and wandered the house, waiting for him to call. She peeked in on Lizzy, who was still sound asleep. Lamia was being oddly quiet, her back turned as she faced the corner. Esme made a cup of tea and clicked on the radio for background noise.

Esme sat on the couch and picked up a book to read, not being able to focus on the words. She set the book down next to her teacup and closed her eyes, hoping things weren't as bad as they feared at the restaurant.

The sound of Lizzy crying woke Esme, and she peered in the dark to see her daughter standing in the doorway, clutching her teddy bear. Esme rubbed her eyes and shook away the cobwebs. "Hey, why are you out of bed?"

Lizzy stared at her. "Where's Daddy?"

"He needed to run to the restaurant for a bit. Are you alright? Do you need something?"

Lizzy appeared unsure and squeezed her bear to her chest. "Is Daddy hurt?"

Esme recoiled, wondering where that question came from. "No, honey, he just needed to check some things out. Why would you ask that?"

"I had a bad dream. Daddy was hurt by a monster," Lizzy replied in her tiny voice.

Esme felt panic seize her chest and tried to breathe through it. Children had bad dreams, not everything was an omen. Maybe she was picking up on her parents' tension about the break-in. "Let's get you back to bed, Lizzy. Daddy will be home soon."

Getting up to guide her daughter back to bed, Esme turned on a light to see better. The light warmed up the room, casting a soft yellow glow into all of the shadows. Lizzy gasped, and Esme glanced to see why. Lizzy's eyes were focused directly on Lamia.

"Mommy, there's the monster in the corner," she cried, her eyes wide with fear.

Not *a* monster, *the* monster.

Lamia had rotated to face them, and her face was twisted in a strange delight. "Lizzy," she hissed, drawing out the "z"s.

Esme immediately stepped between the creature and her child, finding herself needing to protect Lizzy. Lamia crept out of the corner toward them, her face twisted in a creepy grin, and Esme stepped back toward Lizzy.

Lizzy began to scream as Lamia unfurled herself to full height and moved quicker in their direction, a low growl emanating from her chest. Esme grabbed Lizzy in her arms and ran out of the room. She made it to Lizzy's room and hurried in, slamming the door behind them.

The sound of scratching came from the outside of the door, and Esme locked it from the inside, knowing if Lamia wanted to come in, she probably could. Either Lamia was playing a game, or she was being kept out by some unseen force. Esme prayed for the latter.

Pounding started on the door. So hard, it rattled on its hinges. Lizzy began to sob and clung to Esme, trembling. Rage filled Esme as she pictured Lamia on the other side of the door. She pressed Lizzy to her body and yelled. "Go away!"

It fell silent on the other side of the door. Then a deep cackle came through the cracks. "Lizzy," Lamia whispered as if she were luring prey.

The door handle began to rattle, making Lizzy scream in terror. Esme had brought this hell upon her child and needed to end it. She imagined stabbing Lamia over and over until the creature fell into pieces and withered away to nothing. She now understood love for her child and wouldn't let anything happen to Lizzy.

The rattling stopped, then Lamia said the word that made Esme's blood run cold. Lamia pressed her mouth to the door and said, "Pete."

The hall went silent, and Esme understood. Like with Allison, Lamia was going after Pete. She waited a moment, listening for any sounds, then peered into the hallway. It was empty. She crept through the house, but Lamia was nowhere to be seen. She was gone.

Esme knew she needed to get to Pete. To save him. She wasn't sure what Lamia was going to do, but Esme needed to get to him first. She threw on a jacket and covered Lizzy with a blanket. Lizzy had asked if Daddy was hurt. She'd known something then.

They went to Esme's car and she loaded Lizzy up in her seat, buckling her in. Lizzy was sniffling and shaking in the seat. "Daddy?"

"Yes, honey, we are going to get Daddy."

She drove through the quiet city streets toward the restaurant, hoping Pete wasn't alone. Lamia would only go after him if he was. She looked for his car as she drove in case he was on his way back home. She peered down side streets in the off chance he took a different route. As she was doing this, Lizzy began to scream, and Esme jerked her eyes forward.

Lamia was standing in the middle of the road with her long arms spread wide open like she was welcoming heaven into them. Or hell. Her eyes blazed with rage, and her mouth contorted into a strange grimace. Esme didn't have time to stop and yanked the wheel to go around Lamia. This caused the car to careen out of control and hit a telephone pole.

Esme came to with blood pouring out of a gash in her forehead. She frantically looked in the back seat to check on Lizzy. Her daughter was okay, but crying uncontrollably. Lamia was nowhere in sight.

Had she gone for Pete?

Sirens cut through the darkness, and Esme could see the flashing lights coming toward them. How could she explain what happened? Why she was even out with her four-year-old daughter at this time of night? In their pajamas no less. Her brain was too foggy to think, so when the rescuers came to her, she couldn't speak.

Somehow, Pete saw the accident and recognized Esme's car on his way back home. He parked and ran as they were getting Esme out of the car to the ambulance. He took Lizzy from one of the paramedics and came over to Esme. He leaned over her, his eyes searching her face.

"Esme! What happened? Why are you and Lizzy out here at this time of night? Were you coming to the restaurant to find me?" His voice was panicked, and his eyes were confused.

Esme gazed at him, knowing this was the end of the line. She could have killed her child that night. All because of Lamia. The creature that would never leave them alone. She loved Pete and Lizzy too much to let it happen again. Tears poured down her face as she met Pete's eyes.

"There is something you need to know. Something I should have told you a long time ago."

Pete frowned. "What?"

"I see things."

Chapter Twenty-Eight

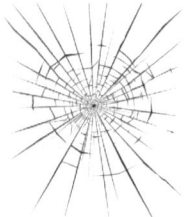

P ete sat quietly as Esme told him in detail about her life. Over their years together, she'd told him only what she was comfortable with, but now he needed to hear everything. Even the parts she was sure he would think she was insane because of. His face was soft and judgment-free while he listened. He nodded or commented neutrally as she spoke to encourage her to open up.

They were home after the accident, and Lizzy was in bed sleeping. The doctor cleared them both to go home, but gave instructions for Pete to keep an eye on Esme as she had a concussion. The accident was ruled no-fault as it was only Esme's vehicle. She told the police the sun had gotten into her eyes, and she thought she saw someone in the road and swerved to avoid them. The female officer was nice and said that could sometimes happen.

So, after a few scans and a row of stitches to close up the gash on her forehead, Esme and Lizzy were sent home with strict instructions to rest. Pete had stood dutifully by his wife's side, letting her statement to him at the accident site wait between them until she was ready to address it.

I see things.

Now that they were home, Esme knew she needed to open up and tell him before she lost the nerve. Lizzy was happy to be home in her own bed and didn't fight going to sleep at all. Once she was bedded down, Esme and Pete sat on the couch, and she began from her earliest memories. Then she talked about Gogo.

"Gogo?" Pete asked, curious. "Did he tell you that was his name?"

"I don't recall." She didn't anymore. She couldn't remember how they even met. Surely he told her that was his name, otherwise, where would the name have come from?

She went on to talk about Tall Man, how her Uncle Ray died, and Aunt Darla changed, withdrew inside of herself. How, sometimes she'd see Uncle Ray hanging around. Then she spoke about Becky stepping up and becoming like a parent to Esme when Aunt Darla checked out.

Pete turned his head. "She sounds nice. I mean, she was nice the night I met her at Linda and Jo's, but we didn't talk much because..."

Because Esme freaked out and ran away. She nodded. "She is nice."

"Why don't you really interact with her now?" Pete asked, not accusing.

Esme shook her head. She'd told him before about her lashing out at Becky at the hospital that day, but had left out more

203

than her being angry and yelling at her cousin. "We had the falling out when she married Mario. Well, really, when I found out about them being a couple and her being pregnant. When she told me at the hospital, I... I acted badly."

"I'm sure it wasn't that bad, Esme. We always remember things worse than they were," Pete whispered.

"I assure you it was. I attacked her," Esme countered, not willing to lie anymore.

"Physically?"

Esme sighed. "Yes. Physically and mentally. Becky has forgiven me now, but I haven't forgiven myself for what I did. I don't trust myself."

Pete fell silent, likely thinking what Esme was, as well. If she couldn't be trusted with an adult, how could she be trusted with Lizzy, a vulnerable child? Esme couldn't answer that because she didn't think she should be. Especially not after the accident.

Lamia would make sure of that.

Pete excused himself to check on Lizzy and put the kettle on. Esme could sense he also needed to step away to gather his thoughts. She couldn't blame him. She hadn't even told him about Marty or Lamia yet.

He came back with two cups of tea a little while later, handing one to Esme. He kissed her on the head, and she was grateful for his gentleness. He might feel differently by the time she was done telling him everything.

Knowing she needed to keep the momentum, she cleared her throat. "When I was in school, they said I killed a girl. That girl Sara I told you about? We didn't just fight that day by the buses. It started that way, but they say I pushed her into the road into oncoming traffic."

Pete stared at her in astonishment, his cup of tea held in midair. "Did you?"

Esme stared into her tea, seeing her own warped, dead-eyed reflection peering back at her. "I guess so. I had this friend Marty who did it."

"So you didn't do it? I don't understand? Did you help her do it?"

"I never saw Marty again."

Pete frowned, trying to piece together what she was saying. "Was she arrested, sent away?"

Esme struggled to bring the conversation clarity. "I saw her push Sara, but with my hands. Sort of. It was like we became the same person at that moment, then she simply disappeared, and it was only me standing there."

Pete tried to keep his face calm, but she saw it. The flash of fear in his eyes. What she was telling him was that she made up a person to kill a classmate. Or, at least, that's how it sounded coming out of her mouth.

He ran his hand through his hair and coughed lightly. "Is that why you were in the hospital before you were at the halfway house?"

Esme nodded, falling silent for a moment. She met his eyes. "Pete, they said Marty never existed. Like Gogo and Tall Man. That I alone committed the crime and killed Sara."

"How long, uh, how long were you in the hospital?"

"From when I was thirteen to eighteen."

She could see him doing a mental tally of the timeline. He set his tea cup down and leaned back against the couch. "They released you, though. So, you must be better, right?"

Esme wanted to cry with the wall of lies crumbling around her. She wanted to just agree with him and go back to their simple life, but that wasn't fair to him or Lizzy. She reached out and touched his hand almost as an apology. "There's more."

Pete looked like he absolutely didn't want to hear any more and grimaced. He pushed his glasses up on his nose and waited. Esme continued.

"In the hospital, I started seeing this creature. She was large with stringy red hair and a twisted jack o'lantern-like face. Long arms and pointed teeth and nails. She lived in my room with me."

Pete failed at hiding his horror but continued to sit quietly and listen. His tea grew cold on the table as he tensed with what was coming next. Esme paused, thinking he'd heard too much when he said hoarsely, "Go on."

Esme told him about how Lamia followed her around and repeated things she said. How when she was sent to the halfway house, Lamia came with her. About the session with Allison when Lamia hit Allison with the watering can. Pete cocked his head at this, understanding more than Esme was telling him.

"Yes, they said it was me, and I remember the watering can in my hands after. See, Pete? I'm messed up inside," Esme explained, tapping her skull.

"What happened next?" Pete asked, not responding to that comment.

"Allison committed suicide in the hospital when she was sent back for attacking the cat."

Pete stared at her, trying to read between the lines. "Is that what happened?"

Esme shook her head. "I don't know. I had an image of Allison in the hospital, cowering in a corner like someone was standing over her."

"Where were you when she died?" Pete questioned, this time a little more accusing.

There it was. Now he was starting to understand.

Esme put her chin up. "I was at the halfway house. We weren't allowed to leave without checking in so they can confirm I was in my room all night. However, something else strange happened."

"What?"

"Lamia disappeared during that time."

"I see. So you never saw her again?" Pete asked, seeming relieved.

This was the hard part. "She came back after I found out Allison committed suicide. I thought she was out of my life. Then, she simply left again. It was like she was done with me. I saw this shadow being afterward until it drew me into a black hole. In there, I saw my purpose, I think. Why I am. Why I exist. I know that sounds crazy, but I thought I could put this all behind me after that. I believed going into the black hole reset things, made me okay again. After that experience, I didn't see things anymore. Not for years."

"Until when?" Pete whispered, dreading the answer.

Lizzy.

Esme cast her eyes down with shame. "When I was pregnant with Lizzy, Lamia came back. She was obsessed with the baby and wouldn't stop."

Pete sat up straight. "Stop what?"

"Stop trying to get to Lizzy. I don't know if she loved or hated her, but she was hellbent on having her. She caused the accident that night."

Pete's eyes flashed with rare anger, and he balled his hands into fists. "What do you mean?"

"She was threatening you. I went to find you, to make sure you were safe, and Lamia appeared in the road in front of the car. I tried to avoid her and hit the telephone pole."

A plethora of expressions crossed Pete's face, and he rose, standing still for a moment. Then, he walked to Lizzy's room, went in, and shut the door. Esme waited for him to come out, but he didn't. Not for the rest of the night.

She slept on the couch and woke up hearing Lizzy in the kitchen in the morning. Pete was making their daughter breakfast. Esme went to the kitchen and watched from the door, wishing she could put everything behind her and enjoy the family she'd been given. Lizzy saw her and waved with a smile.

Pete turned to see Esme and frowned. "Lizzy, Mommy, and I are going to talk for a minute."

Pete guided Esme out of the kitchen, and they stood in the hall. "Lizzy told me what happened the night of the accident. She said she saw something in the road. She also told me that night something scared her in the house, but she couldn't explain what it was. She said you ran with her to her room and locked you both in there. That's terrifying; you need to understand that. To think something was trying to hurt you, to hurt Lizzy. I want to help you, Esme. To find out what is happening. I believe you."

Esme could see the fear in his face and how he was doing his best to protect his family. She couldn't let him sacrifice himself like that. She needed to do what was best for him and Lizzy. She embraced him as tears slipped down her face. She stepped back and shook her head.

"She won't leave you alone as long as I am here."

Chapter Twenty-Nine

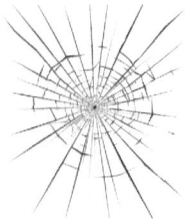

Despite Pete's resistance to the suggestion, Esme knew what she needed to do. The only way she could protect her husband and child was to not be around. To leave their lives and force whatever was following her to forget about them. So she decided to do what was going to hurt them all to save the people she loved.

"I'm having myself recommitted to the hospital," Esme told Pete, not allowing it to be a discussion.

Pete's face contorted in panic, and he took her hand. "No, we can work this out! Get therapy. Move. Whatever it takes. Lizzy needs her mother around. I need my wife, Esme. I love you. I can help you."

Esme could see his heart breaking and felt hers break in return. It would be so easy to agree and pretend it was enough...

but she knew better. This wasn't going away. In fact, it seemed to be getting worse.

What would it take? Lizzy could have died when Lamia stood in front of the car, causing the wreck. Next time, Esme was sure they wouldn't be so lucky. Next time, Lamia would make sure to complete the task. There could be no next time, Esme decided.

"Pete, it doesn't have to be forever. I need to go for now to try and stop what is happening to me. To us. I should have done this a long time ago. It was unfair to you and Lizzy for me to think I could handle this on my own. I can't. I need to be in a place where I can't hurt anyone else."

"Too late," Pete whispered through tears. Esme could see the suffering she'd caused to the one person who loved her for who she was.

Who he *thought* she was.

Esme felt the weight of his hand in hers and thought it felt like an anchor. No, more like cement drawing her underwater. Pete's love was too much for her to carry. Beautiful, pure, heavy. So heavy she couldn't hold it up anymore. She didn't deserve him or Lizzy.

Lizzy came running around the corner to see her parents standing awkwardly in the hall, their faces filled with pain. Very quickly, she scanned their expressions and knew something was wrong.

"Are you mad at me?" Lizzy asked in a tiny voice.

Pete immediately crouched down and gathered his daughter in his arms. "Of course not, honey. Mommy and Daddy are just talking."

"About me?"

Pete glanced at Esme, not sure how to respond. He turned back to Lizzy. "About making sure you are safe."

Lizzy stared at Esme, with eyes much older than her years. "Are you mad at me, Mommy?"

Esme shook her head, fighting back tears. This innocent little girl didn't need to spend her life questioning if she was the reason for her mother's issues. She had the right to an unencumbered childhood.

"No, Lizzy. I'm glad you are alright and that Daddy made you breakfast. Did you finish eating?" She tried redirecting the child.

Lizzy nodded.

Pete stared at Esme for a moment, wanting to say more, then rose and took Lizzy by the hand. "Why don't we go color in the living room?"

Lizzy smiled and hopped up and down. "Will you draw me a puppy, Daddy?"

"A puppy? I can sure try. Esme, do you want to join us?" Pete asked, his eyes seeming distant as he processed the destruction of their little family.

"No, I'm going to grab a shower. Pete?"

He paused and looked at her, the gravity of the future hanging in his expression. It was as if a giant hand was squeezing the life out of them both. They locked eyes for a moment, the hopes of their lives together evaporating before them. Esme couldn't speak, and Pete dropped his head and guided Lizzy to the living room to color. Esme stood alone in the hallway, wanting to rush to him and make it okay.

It wasn't fair.

In the shower, Esme bawled and scrubbed her skin so hard it began to bleed. She wanted to erase herself, replace who she was with a better version of who she was. To scrape off all the messed-up parts and start over. However, nothing she did was going to change to reality she was a detriment to those she loved. Who loved her despite it all.

After the shower, Esme crept to the bedroom and picked up the telephone. Even though any doctors she knew at the hospital were long gone, she was always given the name and number of the next doctor in line in case she needed it. Her therapist on the outside, whom Esme rarely saw, made sure she had a support tree in the chance Esme had a mental breakdown.

Like now.

The phone rang a few times, and a soft-spoken man answered. "Dr. Fishman's office, this is Eric. You are not alone. How can I help you today?"

"Uh, hi. I was given Dr. Fishman's number from Dr. Tidel. Is Dr. Fishman in?"

"He's with a patient at the moment. Can I leave him a message to return your call?"

Esme chewed her fingernail. This seemed like something that a message wouldn't be able to convey the seriousness of the situation. "My name is Esme. He doesn't know me, but I used to be a patient there at the hospital. He's on my support tree in case I needed extra help."

"Do you?" Eric asked.

"Do I what?" Esme replied, confused.

"Need extra help?"

Esme coughed ot cover the tightness in her throat. "I think I do. I think I need to come back."

The line was quiet, and Esme thought Eric had hung up when another voice came on the line.

"This is Dr. Fishman. Is this Esme?"

Esme sat up straight. "Yes. Dr. Fishman, Dr. Tidal gave me your number. I used to be a patient there years ago. I went to a halfway house and then on my own after. I have sort of been going to therapy, but things have taken a turn for the worse."

"How much is sort of?" Dr. Fishman asked.

Esme knew she needed to be honest. "Like every few months or so."

"I see. Can you tell me what is going on with you at the moment?"

Esme felt the gates release and poured out everything, including that she first started seeing Lamia while she was in the hospital. How she lied about what she was seeing and experiencing all along. She was ashamed to admit it all, however, being honest felt like a huge weight was being lifted off her shoulders.

Finally, she told him what happened with Lamia and how she crashed her vehicle seeing the creature in the road. Dr. Fishman listened, and she could hear what sounded like a pencil scratching on paper over the line. Once she finished telling him everything, the line was quiet for a moment, but she could still hear the pencil on the paper.

Dr. Fishman cleared his throat. "Thank you for being honest with me, Esme. I know that must have been very difficult. I have pulled up your files and taken some notes. It does sound like you are having an episode of psychosis and would benefit from some more immersive care. Can you let me know what your intent is with calling me?"

"I... I need help. I'm worried my family will get hurt, and I can't let that happen."

"I can't make any suggestions over the phone, however, what are you asking of me right now? For a referral or something else?" Dr Fishman questioned.

Esme understood the dance. She had to be the one to say what she needed, so it didn't seem like he was coercing her to do something she didn't want to. She caught a glimpse of herself in the bedroom mirror and didn't recognize herself. The stranger in the mirror wearing a bath towel, long wet hair dripping on the carpet. This woman looking back at her, was foreign to her.

"Dr. Fishman, I'm terrified about my family's safety if I am around them. I'd never intentionally harm them, but I feel other things are involved."

"I understand, Esme. I think you are being very brave in recognizing your situation and reaching out for help. How exactly can I assist you today?"

This was it. She needed to say it. To form the words to open the door. "I think I need to be readmitted to the hospital for mental care."

"Okay. What are you wanting to be admitted to the hospital for? Observation? Treatment?"

"Both, everything. I can't do this on my own anymore." The words were possibly the most honest words to ever come out of her mouth. The truth of them releases some of the ties strangling her inside. Tears rolled down Esme's cheeks, knowing she was doing something she should have done long before, but ultimately would make her lose everything that ever mattered to her.

"I am sending over some paperwork to your therapist, Dr Tidel. Once she fills it out and sends it back, we will start the admission process. Although this is voluntary, please understand we will assess your mental state and make a determination for your care based on these findings," Dr. Fishman explained.

"I understand. Thank you for taking my call," Esme replied, feeling a mixture of fear and relief.

"If you feel like you need immediate assistance while we get this process rolling, please reach out to Dr. Tidel or go to the emergency room if you are in a critical situation."

"I will."

They hung up, and Esme sat in her bedroom, not sure how to move her body. She ran her fingers along the rough edge of the towel. She could hear Lizzy giggling in the other room, and her mind struggled with hearing the normal sounds of life, while hers was crumbling all around her. She dressed and walked out to the living room door, catching Pete's eyes for a second. His flashed was concern at the realization of what was going to happen.

He stepped over to Esme and wrapped his arms around his wife. They clung onto each other, not wanting to let go, but knowing it was now out of their control.

Esme moved back and frowned. "I called the hospital."

"You did? What did they say?" Pete asked, knowing the answer.

"I think they are going to admit me. He is reaching out to my therapist to start the process."

Pete tensed, not realizing how quickly everything would happen. "I don't want you to go."

Esme chewed the inside of her lip. Neither did she. "I have to, Pete. It won't be forever. You and Lizzy deserve someone who isn't mentally unstable. She deserves to feel safe."

"You aren't mentally unstable, Esme, you have been dealt a bad hand."

"Pete, don't make excuses for me. I love you, but I need help. I could have hurt Lizzy."

He couldn't argue that and let his shoulders drop, defeated. "I'll come visit."

"I'd like that."

They stood on the precipice of the unknown and tried to make it seem less daunting. They went to where their daughter was drawing and put on happy parent faces.

While they were dying inside.

Chapter Thirty

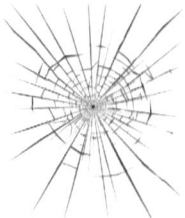

A little had changed at the hospital since Esme's first stay. More color had been added to the walls, and each room was more personalized. Patients were also allowed to bring in approved items from the outside to make their rooms feel more like home and less institutional.

Esme hung up pictures Lizzy drew all around the room, and brought the bedspread from her and Pete's bed to feel close to him. They'd all cried when she left, and she felt like she was letting her family down. Failing them. In reality, she was trying to save them.

To save herself.

She and Dr. Fishman met as soon as she arrived, and both agreed it would be best if she didn't see her family for the first month. To give her time to settle in and address some of the issues she'd been dealing with. However, she spoke to Pete and

Lizzy on the phone every night. She knew she'd left Pete with a lot to handle on his own and was relieved when he told her Jo and Linda agreed to watch Lizzy when he worked. They had been like family since the beginning to her and Pete, and Esme was forever grateful for the two women's presence in their lives.

The first night in the hospital was difficult, and Esme couldn't sleep, crying most of it. She missed her husband, she missed her little girl. Even though she'd had a hard time bonding with Lizzy at first, being away from her made Esme's heart hurt.

Dr. Fishman recommended a regime of Cognitive Behavioural Therapy, anti-psychotic medication, and hypnosis to start Esme's treatment. Though she hadn't seen Lamia yet, she knew the creature was waiting to emerge. Dr. Fishman thought the hypnosis might help Lamia come forth in a controlled environment.

"Things seem different here now," Esme noted, glancing around the therapy room. "Even the treatments are not the same as when I was here as a teenager."

"We constantly try to evolve to meet the needs of our patients. Gone are the days of sterile, white halls and forcing patients into treatments. Our goal now is to work with you to find the best forms of care to help you succeed in your progress. You are a partner in your overall treatment, and we want you to feel comfortable and empowered. Every patient's needs are different, and we try to find what works best for them."

For the first session, Esme was nervous but ready. Dr. Fishman had her rest in a reclining chair as he began the session, starting a metronome. "Relax and let your mind go. Focus on the metronome and listen to my voice as I guide you. You are safe here."

Esme relaxed, finding the environment to be soothing. Dr. Fisman's voice was steady and almost seemed in rhythm with the metronome. Before she realized it, she was in a deep, meditative trance.

She was a small child again, walking through the hall at her Aunt's house. Becky and John were at school, and Aunt Darla was at work. Only Uncle Ray and Esme were home. Uncle Ray was watching television, his feet kicked up in his recliner as he drank a beer. Esme went into the room and sat on the couch.

Uncle Ray smiled at her. "Hey there, Esme. What are you up to?"

"I was playing with my dolls, but I got bored," Esme replied in her tiny voice.

"You want to come sit with me and watch this program? They are fixing up an old house."

That sounded boring, too, but Esme went over and climbed up into the chair with Uncle Ray. For a bit, they sat in silence watching the guy on the TV rip out old walls. Esme began to doze off and woke up to her uncle massaging her thigh. She shook the sleep out of her head. His hand kept making a circular motion on her skin, inching up. Esme felt uncomfortable, but Uncle Ray was always nice to her, so she didn't stop him.

Seeing she was awake, he paused his hand for a moment. Esme was frozen, not sure what to do. Uncle Ray took this as a sign and reached into her panties.

Esme jerked awake in Dr. Fishman's office and sat up, her eyes wide. Her heart was pounding as the memory sat in the forefront of her mind.

Dr. Fishman was watching her and nodded. "Can you tell me what you remember? You were talking to someone named Uncle Ray," he said.

Esme gulped, feeling her throat constrict. "I, uh, he." She stopped, feeling her cheeks flame.

"You did nothing wrong, Esme. You were a small child, trusting adults around you. What did he do?"

"He touched me. He..." Even saying the words made Esme horrified.

"It's okay, take your time. You don't have to tell me if you don't want to. You can write it in a journal instead. However, you need to address it as part of your truth," Dr. Fishman suggested.

The room turned cool, and a shadow appeared behind the doctor. Not Lamia... Tall Man. Tall Man had something to do with Uncle Ray. The shadow moved forward, and Tall Man's eyes bore into Esme's soul. She understood. Uncle Ray had been molesting her, and Tall Man came to protect her. She met Dr. Fishman's eyes.

"Tall Man is here. He was a friend when I was a child. He disappeared after Uncle Ray died. I made him go away because I thought he killed my uncle."

"I see. How did your uncle die?" the doctor asked gently.

"He had a heart attack or something and fell down the stairs," Esme replied, dredging up the memory.

"Do you feel guilty about that?"

"I used to when I was little. Not anymore. He was a bad man."

"Your uncle?"

Esme nodded. "I thought he was nice. I thought he cared about me, but he did things to me."

"Like touching you? Do you remember anything else?" Dr. Fishman asked, waiting patiently for her to work through the process on her own.

Esme shook her head. She didn't want to. "No."

"Do you think Tall Man came to protect you?"

Esme considered that, and it all made sense. She didn't remember Uncle Ray molesting her, but her mind did and brought Tall Man in. She thought he killed Uncle Ray, and maybe he did, but he was only trying to protect Esme. "I think so. I didn't recall what happened, but Tall Man came after I moved in with Aunt Darla and Uncle Ray. After Gogo left."

"Who do you think Tall Man may have represented to you at the time?"

Esme knew. "My father. I remember him sometimes. He was always so gentle and nice to me."

"I see. That's a good point. Let's talk about Gogo, as well. Was Gogo a boy or a girl?"

"A boy."

"Okay, a boy. Gogo was your first friend no one else could see?" Dr. Fishman asked.

"Yes. He also showed up after I moved in with Aunt Darla and Uncle Ray," Esme explained.

"Is he here now?"

Esme glanced around the room but only saw Tall Man. "No, I haven't seen him since they made him go away."

"I see. Can you tell me anything about him? What did he look like?"

Esme remembered how Aunt Darla showed her a picture of her father when he was a little boy. "Also, my father. When he was little. Gogo was a young boy around my age when he started showing up. Later, my aunt showed me a picture of my dad, and it was him. Gogo."

"Ah, but you didn't know that when you saw him at first, correct?"

"No. I don't think so. I mean, maybe I'd seen a picture of my father from then and didn't remember, but when she showed me the picture, I didn't know it was my father," Esme answered, pieces beginning to fall into place.

"Do you think maybe Gogo and Tall Man were manifestations of your father, whom you loved and lost? A way to still feel close to him?" Dr. Fishman asked.

Esme thought about that and stared at Tall Man. Her memories of her father in physical form were only of a tall shadow moving through their house. She could almost bring his voice to memory, but not his face. Only that he was a tall man. She sucked in her breath and saw Tall Man in a new light. He was her protector, her safe place.

Tears ran down her cheeks. "I'm sorry, Tall Man. I'm sorry I made you go away."

Dr. Fishman listened but didn't intervene. Esme stood up and walked over to where Tall Man was. She wasn't able to touch him, but she stood in front of him, her heart aching. "I know you were only looking out for me. Trying to keep me safe. I didn't understand what was happening to me. I thought you hurt Uncle Ray, but now I see you were acting as a buffer between us to try and save me."

Dr. Fishman cleared his throat. "Esme, is there something you would like to tell Tall Man?"

She took a deep, shuddering breath. "I love you, Daddy. I miss you."

Dr Fishman rose and came to stand beside her. "Do you need Tall Man to protect you anymore, or can you now release him?"

Esme stared at her friend, her father, and smiled. "I set you free. Thank you for watching over me, Daddy."

Tall Man stepped forward into Esme, and she felt him become part of her past, her memories, and herself. She fell to her knees, sobbing. Dr Fishman rested his hand on her shoulder.

"I think that's enough for today. I have a workbook for you to start using for Cognitive Behavioral Therapy. I also want you to start journaling and think about your other life companions and what role they may have played in your life. You did really well today, Esme. It's hard to confront the past, but necessary."

Esme got up and blew her nose with a tissue from the desk. She met Dr. Fishman's eyes with a wobbly smile. "Tall Man is part of me now."

He smiled. "That's progress. We'll meet again in a couple of days. Here's the workbook and the journal. Take a few days to write down your thoughts. Reach out to me at any point you need to talk, alright?"

Esme nodded. He was different than the other therapists she'd had in the past. They listened and made suggestions. He challenged her to face herself. She took the books and headed back to her room, feeling exhausted.

After setting the books on the table, she climbed into bed and slept for the next fourteen hours. More than she'd slept consecutively in years. She could sense Tall Man as part of her now and thought back to any memories of her father.

He was kind. He was sad. He was tall. He was gentle. He was calm. She let these memories assure her brain she wasn't alone as she drifted off to sleep. Tall Man was Daddy. So was Gogo, but in a different way.

Were all of her companions manifestations of people in her life, or situational to help make her feel safe when she wasn't? Esme considered this, but it still didn't make sense, as other people were impacted by these beings at times. Lizzy saw Lamia. How could that be possible if it was all in Esme's head? Lamia was the last companion and the most powerful. Gogo was the first and only her friend. No one could see him except Esme, and he didn't hurt anyone. All her other companions had something to do with people dying around her. Gogo was the doorway in. Did that make Lamia the doorway out?

Esme thought back to try and find a common thread between all the visitors over the years. In a way, Gogo was the most dangerous because he allowed her to accept the companions as part of her reality with him. He was part of the key to it all.

So, where was Gogo now?

Chapter Thirty-One

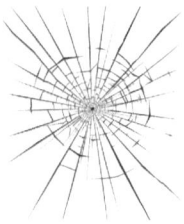

When Pete and Lizzy finally came to visit, Esme was beside herself with terror. She didn't want them to see her differently, and while she had made progress over the last six weeks, she was still far from her goal. She put on a dress and clutched a soft felt bear she'd made for Lizzy. As the time for the visit drew near, she threw up and sat on the toilet, trying to quell her nerves. What if they treated her like a freak? What if Lizzy didn't want to see her anymore? What if her daughter was now afraid of her mother?

A light knock came at the door, and one of the orderlies popped her head in. "Hey, Esme, your family is here in the rec room to see you. You alright?"

Esme stood up and nodded. "No, but yes."

The orderly, Megan, chuckled. "It will be alright. They won't bite."

Esme laughed. "No, but I might."

Megan reached out and touched Esme's arm. "This is a good thing. They seem excited to see you. Well, your daughter is fr sure. She's bouncing off the walls. Your husband looks a lot like you do right now. Jitters."

For some reason, this made Esme feel better. If Pete was nervous, he'd understand why she was, as well. She followed Megan to the recreation room and peered in. Lizzy was running around a table yelling, "Mommy!" over and over. Pete's leg was bouncing up and down as he sat chewing his thumbnail.

Esme came in, and Pete jumped up, his face breaking into a huge grin. They met halfway and embraced tightly, Esme finding comfort in his smell. He ran his fingers down her back and murmured, "I have missed you so much."

Lizzy ran over and practically threw herself at Esme's legs. "Mommy's here!"

Megan excused herself and shut the door so they could be alone. Pete took Esme's hand in his own and squeezed it. "Should we sit down?"

Esme glanced around the room she spent too much time in and shook her head. "There's a little playground in a visitor's area outside. Let's go out there so Lizzy can play while we visit."

Lizzy's ears perked up at the word playground and she jumped up and down with excitement. They made their way out to a small fenced-in area with a playground and picnic tables. Lizzy immediately ran to the slide and climbed up the ladder. This gave Pete and Esme a chance to get comfortable with each other. First, they talked about everyday things like the restaurant and how Lizzy was doing with Jo and Linda.

Once they exhausted the easy chatter, Pete fell silent, then met Esme's eyes. "I'm struggling without you, Esme. I want you to come home so we can be a family again."

Esme stifled a grimace, knowing she was hurting him. "I still have so much work to do here, Pete. It wouldn't be fair to you or Lizzy if I came home before I worked through these things. When I come back, I want to deserve to."

"I know, honey. I just really miss you. I can't sleep without you. However, I want you to get better. Not better, I want you to feel ready. It isn't about deserving, though. You deserve all the good things."

Esme knew his heart was hurting, but couldn't make promises she couldn't keep. She leaned in and kissed him gently. "You are more than I am worthy of, Pete. I *am* making progress here. Addressing things I didn't even know I was dealing with. I promise when I get out, I will be the wife you deserve and the mother Lizzy needs."

Lizzy ran over and climbed into Esme's lap, burrowing her face into her mother's chest. "I miss you, Mommy."

Esme could say she too felt the same. As hard as it was to connect with Lizzy initially, she now missed her daughter every second of every day. She wrapped her arms around Lizzy's small body and sighed. "I'm so happy to see you, Lizzy-bear."

She'd never called her daughter that, but it felt natural to say it. This reminded her of the gift she made for Lizzy, and she picked up her bag. "I have something for you."

Lizzy's eyes grew wide. "You do?"

Esme pulled out the roughly sewn felt stuffed bear and handed it to Lizzy, who acted like she was receiving the best gift in the world. She hugged it to her tiny chest and grinned. "A Mommy bear!"

Lizzy scampered off Esme's lap with the bear clutched close and ran to the playset. Esme watched her, and for the first time, she truly understood what it meant to love someone unconditionally. She and Pete sat in silence as they watched their daughter run across the small bridge on the playset.

Motion caught Esme's eye, and she realized another child was on the playground. That didn't make any sense. The space was only accessible from inside the building, and they had to use a code to get out to it. There were also no other adults around with the child.

The child was partially hidden behind the playset, and Esme frowned. Should she go get someone? Did one of the patient's children get left outside? She began to get up when the child stepped out from behind the play structure and met her eyes with a strange smile.

Gogo.

Esme sat back down hard and caught her breath. Pete glanced around, confused about her reaction. "Are you alright? Lizzy's fine, she's in the tunnel up there."

He thought she'd lost sight of Lizzy and was worried. How could she explain that not only could she see Lizzy, but she could also see her childhood imaginary friend on the playground? No, Dr. Fishman said to call them companions or just friends, as imaginary implied they weren't real, even though they were very real to Esme.

Gogo began scaling the ladder to where Lizzy was, as Esme watched, frozen. He gave her a small wave and continued on up. Once he got to the top, he stepped on the bridge and made his

JULIET ROSE

way over to the tunnel where Lizzy was playing with her new bear.

Relax, Esme told herself. *Only you can see him.*

Pete distracted her by asking her how her sessions were going, and Esme pretended she wasn't seeing Gogo. "Good. Dr. Fishman is using different types of therapy to help me tap into my psyche. It's helping. A lot of what I do is self-guided, like journaling and workbooks. We meet at least once a week, and I go to group sessions every day."

"Do they have any idea when you will be able to come home?" he asked, his words sounding a little stressed out.

Esme shrugged. "Not really. Ultimately, it's up to me when I go home. However, Dr. Fishman has laid out steps I need to take in my recovery, first. I'm working those steps now as part of my treatment."

Pete looked a little disappointed but knew Esme was doing what was best for all of them. "I understand. No pressure, I'm just trying to wrap my brain around how this all works to better help you."

"Thank you, Pete. I know this is hard on you and Lizzy. There will come a time when I move on to another step, which will ask you to come for sessions."

"Me? Why?"

"Once I address my issues and get things under control, you and I will sit with Dr. Fishman so he can also give you tools to help."

"Help you?"

"Help all of us. So if something happens, you know how to handle it. I need to be more honest with you. That was a huge

230

mistake on my part, thinking I could handle this all alone," Esme explained.

Pete wrapped his arms around her and kissed the side of her head. "I'm so sorry, Esme. About everything. I wish I'd known what you were going through. I never want you to feel alone. You can trust me."

"I know, Pete. I was scared about what was happening with me. I didn't want you to think I was losing my mind."

Lizzy chattering on the playset drew their attention, and they looked to see her talking and holding her bear out. To Pete, it looked like Lizzy was speaking to no one, but Esme saw Gogo standing in front of Lizzy. It appeared like Lizzy could see him and was showing him her bear. Esme frowned.

"Lizzy? What are you doing, honey?" she called out.

Lizzy and Gogo turned simultaneously to face her. Lizzy pointed at Gogo. "I'm showing my new friend the bear you made me. My mommy bear."

Esme froze, but Pete laughed. "Your new friend?"

Lizzy cocked her head. "Yes, this little boy. He's my friend, Daddy."

Pete appeared totally confused, but then again, Lizzy often played in her room all alone, pretending she had friends in there with her. "Okay, honey. That's nice. What's your friend's name?"

No, no, no, Esme screamed inside. This couldn't be happening. Lizzy was seeing Gogo, like she'd seen Lamia. If Lizzy was also seeing them, were they imaginary?

Or were they real?

Lizzy whispered something to the boy, and he whispered something back, leaning close to her ear. Lizzy smiled and turned to Pete. "He says his name is Bobby."

Esme furrowed her brow. The boy was most definitely Gogo. Why was he calling himself Bobby to Lizzy? Gogo turned and met her eyes, a sinister grin crossing his face, reminding her of Lamia. A cold chill ran down her back, and she stood up. Something wasn't right. The boy was Gogo, but he also wasn't. He wasn't Lamia either, but something about him was ill-intentioned. Not like the Gogo she remembered. That Gogo was funny and silly, never mean.

Esme took a step forward, trying to keep her cool. "Lizzy, hon, why don't you come sit with Daddy and me for a bit. I'd like to see you before you have to go home."

"We have to leave?" Lizzy asked, her face dropping in disappointment.

"Not yet, little one," Pete replied. "Come see Mommy, though. I'm sure she'd love to hear one of the silly songs you made up."

Songs? Esme was missing out on so much. "Oh, that sounds lovely, Lizzy. Come sing me a song."

Lizzy looked at the little boy, then back at her parents. She clutched the bear with one hand, then put her other hand on the bar to descend the stairs. Esme saw it before she could make it to the playset in time. Gogo's face twisted into a different face, and he stepped toward Lizzy, his eyes unblinking. He raised his hands as she went to go down the first step.

With all his might, he shoved her off the playset.

Chapter Thirty-Two

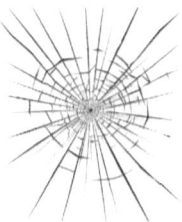

"**L**izzy!" Esme screamed as she ran toward her child. Pete moved faster and had Lizzy scooped up in his arms by the time Esme got to them.

They checked over their crying daughter, but other than being shaken and scraped up, she seemed alright. She bawled and pointed up. "Bobby pushed me!"

Esme glanced up and saw Gogo staring down with a wicked grin. Although he looked like her childhood friend, he didn't act like him at all. Gogo would never have hurt Lizzy. This boy was definitely not Gogo. Esme shook her head and looked back at her daughter. Pete ignored the comment and hugged Lizzy close, his eyes worried and tired.

"Maybe we should go back inside," he said.

Esme agreed and opened the door to let Pete and Lizzy in. Pete set Lizzy on one of the couches and checked her over again.

Satisfied his daughter was not seriously injured, he glanced back out at the playset.

"They really should make sure that's safer for children to play on. I know it's probably not used a whole lot, but it's dangerous. Lizzy could have been really hurt falling off the top of the steps."

He believed Lizzy had slipped and fallen, and Esme wasn't going to correct him. If she said it was Gogo, or Bobby, who pushed Lizzy, he might not come back to visit again, and Esme couldn't handle that. She needed to see her family. "I'll talk to them about that."

They played checkers with Lizzy, who didn't really understand the rules of the game and kept stealing chips off the board. Her giggles were infectious, and she soon forgot about being pushed off the playset. Esme didn't, however, and considered telling Dr. Fishman at her session later that day. How could something her mind made up be seen by her daughter? How could a figment of her imagination push her child? It didn't make sense.

Lamia had crossed boundaries as well, but mostly had used Esme to do so. Except Lizzy had seen the creature, too. It didn't add up. Something was amiss. Maybe Dr. Fishman could shed some light on what was happening.

When it was time for Pete and Lizzy to leave, they all cried and held onto each other. It was wonderful to see them, but their leaving again broke Esme's heart. She promised she'd be home soon, though, now she doubted it was possible. Pete left to use the bathroom before the drive back, giving Esme a chance to be alone with Lizzy.

She crouched down and met Lizzy's eyes. "Honey, do you ever see Bobby or anyone else at home?"

Lizzy wrinkled her nose as she thought. "No. Only when that scary lady was there."

The scary lady. Lamia. When Esme was with Lizzy. "Have you seen her since I came here?"

"No, Mommy. She's scary. I don't want to," Lizzy replied, her voice shaking.

So Lizzy only saw them when Esme was present. Something about them being together made Lizzy able to see and be attacked by what Esme thought were beings she created in her mind. She sighed and hugged Lizzy. "I love you so much, Lizzy-bear. I want you to be safe and happy."

Lizzy rubbed her head against Esme's cheek. "I want you to come home, Mommy."

Esme wanted nothing more than to go home as well, but couldn't risk her daughter's safety. She stood and stroked Lizzy's soft hair. "I know, honey. Hopefully soon. Please keep drawing me pictures and talking to me on the phone until I do, okay? It helps me feel better."

"Okay, Mommy."

Pete came back and saw the distress on Esme's face, assuming it was because they were leaving. He hugged and whispered, "We'll come visit again soon. I promise."

She wanted to tell him not to, that it wasn't safe, but he'd only resist her about it. Smiling, she placed her hand on his cheek. "I love you."

"I love you, Esme."

He let her go and smiled with sad eyes. Scooping up Lizzy, he headed for the door as Megan opened it for him. He gazed back at Esme and mouthed, "I love you" again. She touched her heart and watched her family disappear out of sight. Tears sprang to her eyes, and she went to her room to be alone for a while. By the time she needed to head to her session, she'd bawled until her face hurt.

Dr. Fishman was waiting for her and tipped his head when she walked in. "Are you alright?"

Esme nodded. "My family came to visit today, and it was so hard when they left."

"I'm sorry. Hopefully, they can visit again soon," he offered with genuine concern.

"I need to talk to you about that. I don't think they should come back here," Esme replied, feeling her heart squeeze in pain.

"Oh? Why not?" Dr. Fishman asked with surprise. He took out a pad of paper and laid it on the desk with a pen.

Esme fought back tears. "Something happened today I can't explain. It makes me fear for my daughter's safety. I saw one of my childhood companions."

"One nobody else can see?" Dr. Fishman inquired.

"Yes and no. Gogo. I saw him on the playground with Lizzy, except she could see him, as well. He told her his name was Bobby. He looked like Gogo but didn't act like him."

"I see. They played together?"

Esme stared off. "At first, but when it was time to go, he pushed her off the playset."

Dr. Fishman was quiet for a moment, trying to absorb what she was saying. "You saw him push her?"

"Dr. Fishman, I saw him do it, but so did Lizzy. She also saw Lamia the night we got into the accident."

"Lamia. The creature that you first saw when you came here as a child?"

"Yes."

She could see Dr. Fishman was attempting to wrap his brain around the possibility his patient's child could be seeing imaginary companions. He cleared his throat. "I'll be honest, Esme, if this is true, I don't have an answer as to why."

Did he think she was lying?

"I swear this happened. My daughter was talking to Gogo, whom she called Bobby. She told us he pushed her. I'm not making this up. You can ask my husband"

He leaned forward, his eyes kind. "I don't think you are making this up, but you have to understand from my vantage point, it isn't possible. Now one thing comes to mind. In studies for the Human Genome Project, they hypothesized trauma can be passed from a mother's cells to a baby's cells. Almost like a genetic memory being transferred in utero, if that makes sense. Now, if that's indeed true, some of your experiences could theoretically have been imprinted on your daughter's cells in utero."

"Can that explain how he pushed her?" Esme asked, not sure she comprehended what he was saying.

He sat back and rubbed his chin as he thought about it. "I'm not an expert on the science, but I wouldn't think so. The studies have more to do with psychological imprints. I can't see how that would translate to a physical interaction. Where were you when Lizzy fell off the playset?"

Did he think she pushed Lizzy?

"I was sitting with my husband, Pete, on the bench. We both saw her fall off the playset and ran to her side."

"Did Pete see her get pushed? Did he see Gogo, or Bobby?" Dr. Fishman questioned as his eyes watched her expression when she responded.

"No. Pete thought she slipped and fell. Only Lizzy and I saw what actually happened," Esme explained.

"I'm sorry, Esme, I really don't have a logical explanation at this time. It's possible Lizzy is also experiencing psychosis, however, I can't imagine you would both be experiencing the same visions at the same exact time. It seems illogical."

Esme felt indignant. "Illogical or not, it happened."

He nodded, jotting down some notes. "I'll tell you what, give me a few days to research some historical data and studies to see what I can find on the subject. I can't give you an honest assessment without knowing if this has been recorded in studies. Does that sound fair?"

Esme blew out tension and shrugged in defeat. "I guess so. Please believe me. This happened, Dr. Fishman. I'm not making it up, and don't want anything else to happen to my child. She's been through enough."

"I know you believe it did, and I'm not saying it didn't. I'm a scientist first, and I need to look into the possibility on that level. In the meantime, I would like you to write about the experience today. What you saw, what you were feeling, even sights and sounds. Everything around you. Let's discuss this once I've had a chance to do some research."

Esme agreed and left the room, still feeling like he didn't believe her. She recorded everything she remembered from Pete and Lizzy's visit and brought it back to her session later in the week. Dr. Fishman had done research, as well, and gestured for her to sit so he could share what he learned.

"So, there is a condition called folie à deux, however, it doesn't quite fit your situation. In that scenario, two people can have a shared delusion, but the secondary person is often being isolated or controlled by the main person with the delusion. This isn't your situation, obviously. Did you ever tell Lizzy about your companions?"

"Of course not. I want to protect my child, Dr. Fishman. I would never do anything to put her in harm's way. She only sees them when she is with me, but I never said anything to her or Pete prior to the incidents. I didn't tell him until after the accident about all of this."

"And you said she doesn't see these companions when you aren't around, correct?"

"Yes. So are you saying what I'm telling you isn't possible?" Esme asked.

Dr. Fishman sighed. "I'm not saying it's not possible, but there aren't records I can find in studies of this type of shared psychosis."

"What if it isn't psychosis?"

"What do you mean? Are you asking if it's real?" Dr Fishman questioned, cocking his head.

"Yes. What if the beings are not in my mind?" Esme knew it sounded crazy, but she needed to know.

"Now, Esme, you know that isn't probable. These visitors, according to you, were in the house where you lived with other people, and they never saw them, right?"

"Right."

"Is it more likely you transferred your beliefs onto your child, or that some type of beings come that no one but you can see? Somehow, you are manifesting them and their actions?"

Esme swallowed hard. "Lizzy sees them."

"Again, ask yourself that question?" he nudged gently.

Esme knew at that moment in order to protect Lizzy, she could never see her daughter again. It was the only way to make sure Lizzy and Pete didn't suffer because of her.

Once more, she was alone.

Chapter Thirty-Three

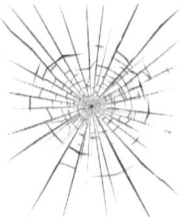

D r. Fishman invited Pete to come for a session so Esme could tell him everything going on with her, including what happened on the playground. Jo and Linda offered to watch Lizzy, as Esme didn't want her there. Not that she didn't want to see her daughter one more time, rather she was afraid for Lizzy's safety.

Pete joined them and sat down, his body tense with anxiety. Esme sat beside him, biting her tongue. Dr. Fishman said he would lead the session to put them both at ease. Pete held Esme's hand as Dr. Fishman began to speak.

"Thank you for joining us today, Peter. We often find when a patient's family is supportive, the patient progresses more. Esme and I have been having sessions one to two times a week since she got here, and there is something she would like to discuss with you after your last visit here with your daughter. Is that alright?"

Pete nodded and glanced between them. "I want to do whatever helps Esme come home."

A look passed between Esme and Dr. Fishman as Esme cleared her throat. "Pete, I have been trying to be transparent with you about what is happening with me. You know about Lamia and the others, but something happened at the last visit I didn't tell you about. Something that scared me, and I have been discussing with Dr. Fishman."

"What?" Pete frowned and squeezed her hand. "You can tell me anything."

Esme wasn't sure he understood what that meant. She shifted uncomfortably in her seat, placing her hands in her lap. "Please don't be upset with me for not telling you sooner, Pete. As you remember, Lizzy said she was talking to an imaginary friend on the playset here?"

"Yeah?"

"I saw him, too."

Pete jerked in his seat, his eyes growing wide. "What do you mean, Esme? How could you see him?"

"Because... it was Gogo. Not exactly. It looked like Gogo but didn't act like him. Do you remember how Lizzy called him Bobby?"

Pete tipped his head. "Yes. She said he pushed her off the playset."

Esme chewed her lip and glanced at Dr. Fishman. The doctor gestured for her to continue. Esme met Pete's eyes. "He did. I saw him do it."

Pete jumped up, agitated, and shook his hands in the air. "That isn't possible, Esme! Imaginary friends don't push people!" He whipped around to face Dr. Fishman. "Tell her that isn't possible!"

Dr. Fishman motioned for Pete to sit down. "I know this is all very upsetting to hear. Esme believes what she is telling you, and we need to address the situation with that in mind. I did some research on Shared Delusion Disorder, however, it doesn't quite explain what happened with both your daughter and Esme seeing the same 'imaginary' friend, as you call it, at the same exact time, doing the same things."

Pete ran his hand through his hair, then pushed his glasses up on his nose. "I'm confused. Are you saying this is a thing? Or it isn't?"

Dr. Fishman smiled and leaned forward. "Both and neither, if that makes sense. Yes, it is a condition, but no, it doesn't quite explain what is happening here. Your daughter says she was pushed by this Bobby child, and Esme says she also saw it happen. As a doctor, I must remain neutral in my analysis of this information, however, I do believe Esme truly feels this is what happened. Without Lizzy to tell us her experience, we can only go off what Esme is telling us. I am here to guide her and you to work through this."

"You expect me to think both my wife and my daughter shared seeing this child, who then attacked my daughter?" Pete asked incredulously.

"Pete, I know this is a lot of difficult information, and I'm not expecting you to believe or not believe it. Esme wanted you here because she *does* believe it happened, and it has made her worried for your daughter," Dr Fishman explained.

Esme could see Pete was about to freak out and placed her hand on his back. "Pete, I am not asking you to believe me. That's up to you. I do need to tell you something, I decided because of it. Something that is going to be hard on all of us, but needs to happen."

Pete glanced at her, his eyes pained. "Esme, I can't take much more. I am burning the candle at both ends. Between running the restaurant and raising Lizzy alone, I don't have much left to give."

This broke her heart. She never wanted to hurt her family. Pete was clearly suffering. "I'm sorry, Pete. You don't deserve this, Lizzy doesn't deserve this. Which is why I wanted to have you come here to tell you."

"Tell me what?"

Esme took a deep breath and tapped into her courage. "I am letting you go. If Lizzy is around me, she's in danger. I'm in treatment, but I don't know how long, or even if, it will work. I'm making progress, but it's not right to have you and Lizzy sitting, waiting for me to come home. I can't leave until I know for sure what is attached to me has been removed."

The emotions that crossed Pete's face twisted Esme's heart. He hung his head for a moment, and when he lifted his face, he was crying. Esme went to put her hand on his, and he pulled it away. "Don't."

Esme stared at Dr. Fishman, who was watching carefully. He spoke softly, "Pete, I understand all of this is a shock, and not what you were hoping would happen here. You have every right to feel the way you do. Esme is only doing what she thinks is best for you and Lizzy."

Pete's eyes flashed up. "What do you know about what's best for my family? Esme came here to get help, and now she is saying she may never leave! Things have gotten worse, not better!"

Dr. Fishman nodded and sat back in his seat. "It certainly can appear that way, however, there are many factors to consider in a patient's overall improvement and treatment. Would you like me to step out so you can talk?"

"No," Esme said.

"Yes," Pete said.

"Tell you what. I will be right outside the door. I think you two need time to speak about this. Knock on the door if you would like me to come back in."

He rose and left the room. Esme glanced at Pete to see him staring at his hands. Part of her wanted to say never mind, and they could go back to being a family, but she knew the companion visits would only increase and become more violent. Lamia went after Pete, and Bobby went after Lizzy. The companions wanted her family out of the way so they could completely control her. If she didn't safely remove them, the companions would see to it another way.

"Pete, I want you to know I love you and Lizzy more than life itself. I have missed you every day I've been in here. I was hoping it would all resolve, and I could come home. Some things have gotten better, some have gotten worse. I want nothing more than for you and Lizzy to be happy. I truly believe I am in the way of that."

Pete gazed at her with red-rimmed eyes. "I love you, Esme. I want you in my life. I can wait until you work through things here."

"I love you too, Pete. That's why I have to insist on this. Imagine how I would feel if you or Lizzy got injured, or worse, because of me. I can't risk it. It's because I love you that I am asking you to let me go."

"What does that mean, 'let you go'? Like not visit?"

Esme shook her head. "It means never see me again. Take Lizzy and start your life over. Meet someone who can be a mother to Lizzy. She's young enough; she'll eventually forget me. Just let her know I always loved her."

Pete began to sob, his shoulders shaking. "I can't do that, Esme. You're my wife, you're her mother. For better or worse, remember? We promised each other that. I can handle this. I just need you home."

"I remember. It's not enough, Pete. I would die if anything happened to either of you. Please understand, I don't want to do this, but it's the only way."

They sat in silence for a moment when Pete came over and kneeled in front of Esme, placing his head in her lap. She ran her fingers through his hair, remembering the young man who took her on her first ever date. How could she do this? How could she never see him again?

The pain in her made Esme feel like she was slipping outside of herself, back into the black hole. She could see it forming before her and pulling her in. Pete didn't seem to notice, and she held onto him as she was drawn further into the abyss.

Suddenly, she was falling, no longer in the therapy room or in the hospital. Pete was gone, and Esme was screaming, attempting to grasp onto anything in the tunnel. Thorns from nowhere reached out and cut her arms as she tumbled past. Scary voices yelled at her from the darkness, and she looked down to see she was a child again, her knees socks falling down her legs to her ankles.

Faces whizzed past her, some familiar, most not. The common denominator is that they were all judging her. *Bad girl. Bad mother. Bad wife. Bad person.* Esme begged them to stop tormenting her, but this only made them louder and more angry. She was being punished for simply existing.

At the end of the tunnel, she landed in a pool of water as large as the ocean and struggled to keep herself afloat. She lashed out, her hands flailing as she slipped under. Water filled her lungs, and she was dragged deeper and deeper into the thick, black liquid.

As she was ready to take her last breath, a strange pulse ran through her body, and she found herself being rocketed back out of the water and through the tunnel. She felt the pulse again, and bright lights surrounded her.

Was she dead?

"Esme, can you hear me?" a voice called out to her. Her eyes stung with the lights as she blinked rapidly, trying to let them adjust. Her body vibrated, and she found she was pinned to some sort of platform.

"Where am I?"

"Esme, this is Dr. Fishman. You are okay. You had a severe psychotic break. We had to use electroconvulsive therapy to bring you out of it. You are here with me at the hospital."

"Pete?"

There was silence for a moment. "Listen to me carefully. You had a psychotic episode. Nothing was working to bring you out of it. You were hurting yourself and others. You attacked Pete,

Esme. I'm sorry. He has left," Dr. Fishman explained, his voice low and kind.

Esme stared at the distorted face of the doctor, glancing around the room. She was strapped to a table next to a machine. That must be how they gave her the treatment. Her body felt odd, and she wiggled her fingers. "I hurt Pete?"

"Yes. He said you started screaming and lashing out, injuring yourself. He tried to settle you down, so you turned on him, hitting and scratching him. We rushed in and pulled you off of him as he was trying to shield himself without hurting you. I'm sorry, Esme. He agreed not to come back. He didn't want to, but he now understands how fragile your healing is."

Esme wanted to die. Nothing in this lifetime made her want to stay in it. She lost her parents, her cousin, Pete, Lizzy. She had nothing to live for. From the corner came a sound, and Esme saw Lamia hovering there. She knew Esme was alone and was preying on her vulnerability. Esme jerked against the restraints and screamed.

"Kill me!"

Chapter Thirty-Four

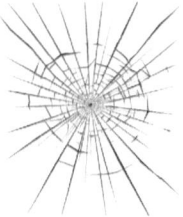

W hatever progress Esme had made over the months prior to that day was dashed into nothing after she attacked Pete. An attack she didn't even remember and hated herself for committing. She hoped he would never forgive her and forget she ever existed. Nothing mattered to her except his and Lizzy's happiness.

As if her wish came true, Pete stopped calling or contacting her. Over the next few years, she'd receive an envelope once a year with pictures of Lizzy as she grew, but that was all. No notes, no cards, no personalization. Esme had pushed Pete away, and he listened.

For Esme, hospital life became her new reality. She would make a step forward and then take a step or two back. Never forward enough to regain control over her mental state. In addition to being shadowed by Lamia, Esme's heart was broken.

Not in the hopeful way that it could be mended, rather crushed to dust so that she stopped caring about anyone or anything. It was easier to let the psychosis take her than to face the reality of what she did to the people she loved most in the world. She stopped trying, and eventually, no treatment worked long-term. Dr. Fishman tried different therapies, eventually understanding his patient wouldn't get better if she didn't want to.

So this went on for decades until she was a strange, old woman wandering the halls of the hospital. Doctors came and went, and all of them tried their best with new and old treatments, but Esme needed to be a partner in her care, and she wasn't. She'd given up. They all learned what Dr. Fishman did. Esme was no longer fighting for herself.

She simply waited to die.

One day, when Esme was in her sixties, she was informed she had a visitor. She hadn't had a visitor in years. A few times, many many years ago, Becky attempted to see Esme, but Becky usually left in tears, and Esme forgot about her cousin the moment she stepped out of the door.

Esme was brought into the rec room, this time with a monitor to watch over, considering her past violence. A young woman sat in a chair at the table, nervously chewing her fingernails. Esme paused and watched the woman, feeling like she knew her from somewhere a long time ago. The woman observed her approach, her eyes guarded and sad. Pete. The woman reminded Esme of Pete. An odd, now unfamiliar pang hit her heart, and she winced.

The woman stood up. "Mama?"

Esme froze. She peered deeply into the woman's face and understood why she was seeing Pete in there. This woman was

Lizzy, her daughter she'd cast away so many years before to protect her. Esme frantically scanned the area, but Lamia was nowhere to be seen.

Was Lizzy safe there?

"Please come sit with me, Mama. I need to talk to you about something important," Lizzy whispered, her large brown eyes pleading. Pete's eyes.

"Is Pete here?" Esme asked, expecting him to pop out of nowhere, looking like he did thirty years prior.

Lizzy shook her head. "No, Mama. It's only me."

Esme sat across from her now-grown daughter and wondered where all the years had gone. She hardly had any memory of the time. Once she was young, then she was old. The rest in between was merely blurry filler. Lizzy was beautiful and carried herself so much like Pete, Esme couldn't stop staring.

Lizzy cleared her throat. "I needed to come tell you face-to-face. Daddy died. He had a heart attack a few weeks ago. He was cremated per his wishes."

Pete was dead? Esme felt her head separate from her body and began to moan. Years of longing surfaced, and she felt her soul retreat from itself. The monitor stepped forward to check on her.

"Esme, do you need me to call the doctor?" he asked.

She continued to moan and started to rock back and forth as the pain exploded inside her heart. "Pete, Pete, my love. What have I done?"

Lizzy touched her hand. "You didn't do anything. He told me everything. How you pushed us away to protect me. I wanted to come visit you so many times, but he told me you wouldn't want me to, that you were worried for my safety. I had to come now, though, and tell you about Daddy. He loved you so much, Mama. He never stopped caring about you."

Esme began to wail, something she hadn't done for years, and it hurt. It was like acid running out of her pores. She dropped to the floor and kicked her legs as she clutched her arms around her chest. Lizzy stared at the monitor helplessly, who radioed for help.

A few moments later, two orderlies came in and picked Esme up off the floor, ready to carry her from the room. Lizzy jumped up, breaking her shock, and put her hand up. "No, please stop. Let me talk to her."

They froze, half holding the weeping, inconsolable woman. Lizzy gestured to the couch. "Rest her there. Let me sit with her."

Confused, they did as they were told, and Lizzy followed behind them. Esme formed herself into a tight ball on the pleather couch, and Lizzy crouched down next to her.

Esme opened her eyes and stared into her child's own pained eyes. "Lizzy."

"It's me, Mama." She began to stroke Esme's tangled hair. "I'm here. It's okay. You aren't alone anymore. Daddy wanted me to make sure you were taken care of. I am taking you with me. Daddy left money in his will to make sure you were cared for. I got you a little house of your own, and I'll visit you every day. This was Daddy's wish in the case of his death. He knew you wouldn't want to live with me, so he left money for you to have a home of your own."

Esme closed her eyes and tried to go back in time. Back to when she had hope. Lizzy continued to rub her head and talk softly to her. Esme felt like a baby being cared for by its mother and relaxed. Lizzy's voice was soothing, and Esme remembered what it was like to be nurtured.

When she opened her eyes later, she realized she had dozed off. Lizzy was gone, if she'd ever been there. Perhaps it was only a cruel dream. One of the monitors was reading a book in a chair by the door and glanced up when Esme stirred, setting their book down.

"There you are. You fell asleep, so your daughter let you rest while she finalized your release. She's meeting with the doctor. She should be back soon."

Lizzy had been there? It *was* real?

Esme rose from the couch and stretched her tired bones. She shuffled to the door, and the monitor stood to let her through. He followed her to her room and paused as she made her way in. She sat on the bed and stared at the wall.

A bit later, Esme heard a knock on the door, and Lizzy and Esme's most current doctor, she quit learning their names after Dr. Fishman left, came in. Esme watched as they walked into the room and took seats facing her. Dr. Whateverhernamewas smiled and made the face Esme hated. The *I care about you because I'm paid to* face. Very condescending and made Esme feel like she was stupid.

"Esme, your daughter has agreed to take over your care and act as your guardian. Isn't that exciting?"

Esme sat still, not wanting to engage. The doctor patted Lizzy on the shoulder and nodded. "You're leaving with her today. Since she lives in a one-bedroom apartment, she has arranged care and housing for you. You can pack up your things and leave with her today. We have set up outside services for you, including therapy and medication delivery. I think you will do as well, if not better, outside these walls than you have for years inside here. Your daughter agrees and is willing to try to let you live your days under her guidance. How does that sound to you?"

Esme shifted her gaze to Lizzy and said the one word that still hung between them. "Bobby."

Lizzy frowned, then her eyes lit up. "I remember. Mama, Bobby, nor anyone else can hurt me. I'm not a child anymore. They have no power over me, do you understand? This is my life, I won't allow them to hurt us again."

Esme wanted to believe her, to finally be free of the torment she'd endured her whole life. The beings who robbed her of her life. Lizzy seemed so sure about everything. Esme nodded. "Okay."

Lizzy smiled, but not in a boisterous way. Like a secret between them. She leaned forward and wrapped her arms around the mother who'd pushed her away. "I love you, Mama. You are coming home."

Within an hour, all of Esme's belongings were placed into a satchel, and she was following Lizzy out into the free world. They drove through the city to a little house in a little neighborhood. Lizzy pulled into the driveway and turned to her mother.

"This is from Daddy. He said he always wanted to give you a home of your own again. He hated you were locked up in that place and always planned for the day you would return to us. He waited for you every day."

Esme stared at the tiny home with its picket fence and rose bushes. Pete never gave up on her. She let tears roll down her cheeks and pressed her fingers to her lips. "Did he remarry? Do you have any brothers or sisters?"

Lizzy shook her head. "No. Daddy worked hard and stayed busy, but he never had another family. You were his wife, and that was enough for him. He talked about you all the time. How beautiful and smart you were. You are."

Hearing that made Esme crumble inside. All those beings stole Pete from her. Stole her from herself. She shoved the car door open and got out, taking a moment to take in what she'd been given by the man she would love for the rest of her days.

Esme moved slowly to the door as Lizzy followed. Lizzy unlocked the door and pushed it open. Inside the home was decorated in all of Esme's favorite colors. Each room was made just for her. She marveled at the attention to detail and felt she didn't deserve what Lizzy had done for her.

What Pete had done for her.

A hiss came from the corner behind her, and Esme turned to see Lamia leering in the corner, drool dripping from her teeth as if she was ready to kill her prey. Esme cringed at the sight of the creature and realized her curse had followed her. No matter where she went, the monsters came along.

Lizzy was pointing out the drapes, which had Esme's favorite flower, poppies, stitched with shimmering golden thread. Esme glanced between her daughter and the creature who never let her go.

Esme walked over to the drapes and let her fingers run across the delicate thread. "It's beautiful."

"Beautiful," Lamia cackled, setting her large presence in the house.

Esme thought back to what Lizzy said about Bobby, how she wouldn't allow him to take over her life. She turned to Lamia, whose face shifted between a creature, a young classmate, an imaginary friend, a shadow, a mirror. Esme understood and walked up to the large creature, leaning as close as she could to the startled being.

"You are done here. This is my home. Get out."

Epilogue

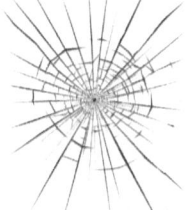

Not all stories have happy endings. Some simply end. Esme lived out her days in her little home, with Lizzy coming most mornings as promised to spend time with her mother. The neighborhood children, convinced she was a wicked witch, mocked and ridiculed Esme whenever she stepped out of her house. Like the beings who tormented her throughout her life, Esme learned to ignore them, to not give them undeserved presence in her life.

One morning after some of the older children pelted her windows with eggs, Lizzy arrived to see the disgusting, gelatinous goo dripping down the panes of glass. She frowned and went inside to check on her mother. Esme was making coffee in the kitchen.

"Mama, who did that to your windows?"

Esme peered at the front windows and squinted, waving her hand dismissively. "Those children."

"What children? You mean the neighborhood kids?" Lizzy asked, shocked. "How long has this been going on?"

Esme shrugged and poured her coffee, ignoring the question. "Would you like some, dear?"

"Mama? Are the neighborhood children being mean to you?" Lizzy pressed.

Esme smiled and sat at the small dining table with her steaming coffee. "I hear it's supposed to rain all week."

Lizzy huffed and turned around. "I am washing that off before it sticks. Mama, you can't let them treat you that way. It's not right."

Esme sipped her coffee like they were having a different conversation and nodded. "Thank you, honey. It will be good for the roses."

Lizzy shook her head and went out to hose the egg off the house. While she was out there, she approached the adults she could find and addressed the treatment of her mother. They all seemed genuinely surprised the old witch had a child, but smiled and promised to speak to their children.

After that, the jeers retreated to whispers and furtive glances behind Esme's back, instead of open taunting to her face. Esme didn't notice either way. She shuffled back and forth to her mailbox and flowers, ignoring the beings outside who treated her like a pariah.

She also ignored the beings inside the home who tried to control her, get her attention, and make her feel less than. Some were old, some were new, all were nothing to the old woman. She moved past them trying to upset her, attempting to break her down. Eventually, one by one, they faded away, and Esme was alone.

Not lonely, simply at peace.

When she finally took her last breath, she saw the one being she'd been waiting for, the one who believed in her all along. She was young again, full of life. Her bones no longer hurt, her mind no longer muddled or tortured. She wandered toward the figure, her heart full. The figure opened its arms and drew her in. Pete kissed her head and held her close as they dissipated out of the world that never accepted her.

She was home.

Acknowledgements

Resources

www.ingramcontent.com/pod-product-compliance
Lightning Source LLC
Chambersburg PA
CBHW030656260626
47157CB00007B/2684

*9 7 9 8 9 9 3 3 7 1 7 0 2 *